Pier Pressure Large Print Edition

An Olivia Morgan Cruise Ship Mystery

Wendy Neugent

SWH Media, LLC

For my mother, Sharol.

Thank you for reading to me every night

when I was a child.

1

"**O**livia, I've made a terrible mistake." Peter reached out his arms, waiting for Olivia to run to him.

A blue sky had greeted Hayley and Olivia as they had walked off the gangway of their cruise ship. Olivia shivered at the sudden drop in temperature as a dark cloud passed in front of the sun, covering them in its shadow.

Olivia froze. Her cheeks flushed pink in the tropical sun. She took a deep breath of the humid air, filled with the briny scent of the ocean water.

"Olivia?" Peter glanced up at the massive cruise ship docked next to them.

Her eyes darted towards her best friend, Hayley.

Hayley shrugged, her eyes wide.

"Peter." Olivia clenched her jaw. "What are you doing here?"

"I shouldn't have left." Peter shoved his hands in the pockets of his shorts and looked down at the ground.

Olivia's heart beat so hard she wondered if he could see it pounding beneath her sundress. She crossed her arms.

"What are you doing here?"

"I'm here to sign back on the ship."

"Things didn't work out with Candi?"

Peter's jaw dropped, and his eyes darted around, avoiding Olivia. "Oh, you know about her?"

"Sure do." A breeze blew her skirt. She reached down to keep it from blowing up.

Hayley touched Olivia's shoulder. "I'm going to give you two some privacy. If you need me, I'll be over on that bench."

Olivia nodded at Hayley, but didn't take her eyes off of Peter. He shuffled his feet.

Olivia waited.

Peter glanced at her before looking back down at the concrete dock. He took a deep breath. "Look, can't we just forget that this past week happened and go back to normal?"

Olivia let out a thin gasp of a laugh. "Ha! Normal? You mean when I was living in ignorance that you were a lying, cheating....."

"Come on, babe. We're good together. I just made a mistake."

"A mistake? A mistake is when you grab the wrong carton and pour orange juice on your cereal instead of milk." Olivia clenched her fists. "It's not cheating on your girlfriend, who is also your business partner, and then abandoning her on the cruise ship with a show scheduled in less than a week."

Olivia walked away from Peter. He followed her and put his hand on her shoulder. Olivia whipped around. "Keep your hands off of me."

"Liv. Don't be like this. I said I made a mistake. I love you, baby. Come on. We're so good together."

"I am not your baby. Never call me that again. As a matter of fact, don't ever call me anything again. We are done." Olivia glared at Peter.

Peter ran his hand through his dark, thinning hair. "Ok, don't be so sensitive. Everyone makes mistakes. What we have is really good."

"I thought it was good at the time, but in hindsight, it wasn't very good at all."

"Ah, baby..." Peter caught himself. "Sorry. Olivia. What do I have to say to you for you to get past this?"

Olivia looked at Hayley sitting on the bench, waiting for her. "Peter. There isn't anything you can say. This past week has been eye-opening for me. I've learned a lot about myself, and one thing I have learned is that I don't need you. I am a perfectly capable woman all on my own."

"What about our show? You need me for that. It's not like you can do it on your own."

"There is no 'our' show anymore."

The wind died down, leaving the air heavy.

Olivia smoothed her skirt. A trickle of sweat ran down her forehead. She wiped it away from her eyes.

"I can get another assistant. But what are you going to do without me?" Peter rocked on his heels and crossed his arms. "You need me way more than I need you, Olivia."

"Ha! Is that what you think? Interesting." Olivia crossed her arms. "I seemed to have done just fine this past cruise without you."

"What do you mean? You did fine without me? Did you get a job as cruise staff or something?" Peter's brows knit together.

"No. I didn't get another job on the ship." Olivia stood up tall, her shoulders pushed back. "I mean, I performed my show for the audience."

"Your show? You don't have a show." Peter scoffed. "You're just my assistant."

Olivia took a deep breath and slowly let it out. "You know, a week ago, I would have agreed with you. But it turns out that I'm not just your assistant. I learned that I can do this without you."

Peter shook his head. "I'm sorry. I really don't understand. Are you saying you performed our magic show without me?"

Olivia nodded. "Yes, that is exactly what I mean."

Peter snorted and shook his head. "That must have been really something. Does Tristan have a new act scheduled to come on today to replace you?"

"No. He liked what I did. I'm finishing out the contract."

Peter tilted his head and laughed. "Oh, I get it. You're sleeping with the cruise director."

Olivia's eyes blazed, and her mouth hung open. "You have got to be kidding me. No, I'm not sleeping with him. I put on a really good magic show. We got a standing ovation."

"We?" Peter raised his eyebrows.

"Yes, we. Hayley, Chico and I."

Peter glared at Hayley. He snorted. "So Hayley saved you, huh?"

"No Peter. I saved me. I am done with this conversation." Olivia walked towards Hayley.

Peter followed her. "I'm going to talk to Tristan and get him to sign me back on.

When he does, we'll discuss whether I'll keep you on as my assistant or not."

Olivia nodded towards the ship. "He's coming down the crew gangway right now. Here is your opportunity."

Peter stormed towards the gangway.

Olivia sat next to Hayley on the bench. She looked up at the clouds racing across the sky.

Hayley took a deep breath and let it out. "Did you take him back?"

Olivia's eyes widened. "Are you kidding me? You think I would take that sorry excuse for a man back?"

Hayley smiled. "When I asked you what you would do if he came back, you said you didn't know. You didn't want to waste all the years you had invested in your relationship with him."

"Yep, you are right. I said that. But now, I know who he is. I'm not throwing good years after bad."

Hayley took Olivia's hand and squeezed it. "Good for you, sis."

Peter walked towards them, sweat trickling down his red forehead. "Hayley, can you give us a minute?"

Hayley stood up. "No, Hayley is welcome to stay." Olivia stood up and grabbed Hayley's arm.

"Fine." Peter clenched his fists. "Tristan said that he and the entertainment director want you to finish the contract."

Olivia looked at Hayley and grinned.

Peter shifted uncomfortably. "So, I guess you need to go on the ship and fill out the paperwork to sign off my illusions."

"Your illusions?" Olivia tilted her head. "The ones you left on the ship?"

"Well, of course. You didn't think you were going to keep all of my stuff, did you?"

"We bought all the props for the show together. For our show. It is not all yours, Peter."

"I bought it all for my career."

"With the money we made doing our show. I'm not just giving it all to you. It's just as much mine as it is yours."

"I will get my illusions back and that bird, too." Peter pursed his lips.

Olivia shook her head. "Chico is my parrot. I paid for him with my money that I inherited when my dad passed. My name, and only my name, is on his paperwork."

Peter's nostril's flared. "Fine."

Olivia stood up and put her hands on her hips. "I'll sign off half of the magic equipment next week. Come here and it will be waiting for you on the dock. You can arrange your own shipping."

Peter opened his mouth to answer and then closed it again. "You can expect to hear from my attorney."

He turned away and walked down the dock towards the terminal.

Olivia sank down onto the bench. She shifted and pulled her skirt down to keep her thighs from getting scalded on the hot metal.

"He never said he was sorry. He never said he loved me." Olivia sighed. "I feel so stupid that I didn't see who he was before."

Hayley put her arm around Olivia's shoulders. "You weren't stupid. You trusted him."

Passengers heading home filled the enclosed walkway coming off of the ship. Crew, heading out to run errands before they had to be back on the ship for the next cruise, streamed off the crew gangway and across the dock towards the terminal.

Olivia rested her head on Hayley's shoulder.

She jolted upright.

"We just lost half of our show. What are we going to do?"

"We'll figure it out. He can't get Chico, that's all that matters. Anything else we will figure out."

Olivia's knee bounced up and down. "I can't believe he was going to take my parrot. He didn't even want Chico. He said that it would be too complicated to travel with a bird. I had to beg him to let me adopt him."

Hayley squeezed Olivia's hand. "You handled yourself really well with him."

Olivia slouched down on the bench and rubbed her face with her hands. "I need to go talk to Tristan and see if he can get a new act by the end of the cruise. We can do the show this week. Then I'll have to give Peter all of 'his' magic equipment. There's no way I could do a forty-five minute show with what will be left."

Hayley rubbed Olivia's back. "Is that what you want to do?"

"No!" Olivia jerked upright. "I don't know. I can't do the show with half of the illusions. It'll be a disaster."

"No, it won't. If you want to do the show, we'll figure it out. We'll do more stuff with Chico. Gail said she loved his part of the show and she'd love to see more of it. If the entertainment director says to add more of your parrot, you should totally add more of your parrot."

Olivia sat up. "You're right. She said that. But, we can't train him to do 20 minutes' worth of new tricks in one week."

"No, but we can go through what we have and see what we can do. If you want to stay on the ship, I know we can make it work."

The ship gleamed as the sun peaked through the clouds and hit its freshly painted side.

O livia perched on the edge of her large black trunk. The metal edge was cold on the back of her legs. Her eyes adjusted from the darkness of the wings to the brightness of the stage lights.

Hayley danced across the stage with five backup dancers in perfect synch behind her. The stage lights bounced off her hot pink sequined gown, sending pink flashes of light around the stage. A pink feather fell to the stage from Hayley's headdress.

Hayley stood in the center of the stage, a spotlight trained on her face, and belted out the last note.

Olivia's hair blew back from the rush of air as the red velvet stage curtains crashed closed in the center of the stage. Hayley waved at Olivia as she and the dancers ran backstage to the dressing room.

The stage crew sprung into action. One crew member pushed a broom across the stage, sweeping up the loose feathers. Two stage crew members push the set off stage and pulled a tall staircase to the center of the darkened stage. They lined the corners of the staircase on the small glowing pieces of tape on the black stage floor, locked the castors in place, and ran into the wings.

Hayley's dance shoes didn't make a sound as she ran out of the dressing room. She paused and pulled the soft covers off of her tap shoes and ran up to the top of the stairway. Her backup dancers followed, posing on alternating steps of the stairs. Hayley's toe tapped in time to the song as she looked up at the dimly lit strip lights. Hayley and the dancers quieted and froze in place.

Olivia held her breath as the music changed. The curtains opened and light flooded the stage. Hayley and the dancers burst into motion as they slowly danced down the stairs, one step at a time, clicking their shoes against the steps, making music from the taps.

Hayley's voice rang through the theatre over the sounds of the audience's applause.

Hayley nodded at Kate. Kate launched into her solo. The sound of her taps echoed off the metal stairs. She tapped across the stair and slid.

Kate tried to catch herself, but her foot slipped out in front of her and she landed hard on the step. She bounced on her bottom to the next step. The audience gasped as she knocked into Rachel, the dancer in front of her.

Rachel tried to avoid Kate by leaping to the right, but her foot slid on the step and she tumbled down the stairs.

Hayley, Mary, and Sara danced to the apron of the stage, and the curtain quickly closed behind them.

Fernando, the stage manager, raced onto the stage and knelt down next to the injured dancers laying at the bottom of the stairs. He helped them up and supported them as they hobbled backstage.

Kate grimaced in pain as she passed Olivia. Olivia hopped off the trunk and followed them to the dressing room.

"Fernando, do you want me to get ice?"

"Yes, and call Dr. Kohli."

"Got it." Olivia raced to the purser's desk. "Sophie! Two of the dancers just fell on stage. I need ice. Can you call Dr. Kohli and tell him to come to the girl's dressing room?"

Sophie's eyes widened as she grabbed her radio off her belt. "Dr. Kohli,

This is the Chief Purser. There is a medical emergency backstage in the girl's dressing room."

Sophie disappeared into her office and came out with a small plastic bucket of ice. She reached under her desk, pulled out two plastic bags, and handed them to Olivia.

Olivia sprinted to the dressing room. She put the bucket on the makeup counter and poured the ice into the bags.

Kate sat next to her, her face contorted in pain. Olivia knelt down in front of her and put the ice on her ankle. It was already swelling and turning colors.

Rachel passed on the ice. "I'm ok. It just shook me up." Rachel rubbed her foot and then flexed it. She got up and took a couple of tentative steps. She looked back at Kate and blew her a kiss. Then she limped through the dressing room door to the backstage.

"Sophie paged Dr. Kohli. He should be here any minute." Olivia put the second bag of ice on Kate's ankle.

The dressing room curtain whipped open and Alex Ballas, the security officer, burst in. "Sophie messaged that there was a medical emergency?"

Olivia looked up at him. "Kate fell down the stairs. I asked Sophie to page Dr. Kohli, not you."

Alex grunted. "Protocol."

Dr. Kohli walked through the dressing room door. "Ah, Kate. Let's see what we have going on with your foot." He knelt down and gently manipulated her foot and ankle.

He put his hands on his knees and sighed. "I can't know for sure until we do an X-ray, but I am concerned we have a break, or at the very least a serious sprain."

Kate burst into tears, thick streaks of mascara streamed down her cheeks.

Dr. Kohli stood up and patted her shoulder. Kate leaned into him. He pulled his radio off of his belt. "We're going to need a wheelchair in the ladies' dressing room, please." Static made the response unintelligible as Dr. Kohli put his radio back on his belt.

The cruise director, Tristan Waterson, raced in, followed by a steward with a wheelchair. "What happened? Did a wave knock you off balance?"

Kate tried to answer, but he couldn't understand her through her sobs.

Olivia volunteered. "Kate was tap dancing down the stairs and slipped. She knocked into Rachel and they both fell to the bottom of the steps."

Tristan glanced at Olivia and nodded. "Dr. Kohli, what is the prognosis?"

Dr Kohli patted Kate's shoulder again. "I can't say for sure until she gets an X-ray, but I fear she has a break, or a bad sprain."

Tristan closed his eyes and dropped his head.

Dr. Kohli and Alex helped Kate get into the wheelchair. "I'll take her to the clinic and do a more thorough examination."

Tristan nodded. "Thank you, Dr. Kohli."

Tristan looked at Olivia. "Where is Rachel? You said she was involved?"

Olivia nodded her head towards the stage. "She didn't think she was hurt. She went back out on stage."

"Dr. Kohli, I'll send Rachel down to your clinic after the show. I want you to make sure she isn't hurt. Let me know if you clear her for the next show."

"Of course." Dr. Kohli pushed Kate towards the door.

"I'll bring you Dr. Kohli's report, Tristan."

"Thanks, Alex."

"Kate, is there anything I can do for you?" Olivia asked.

Kate shook her head. "I can't even think right now."

"If you think of something, let me know. Okay?"

Alex glanced at Olivia and followed Dr. Kohli and Kate out of the dressing room.

Tristan cocked his head towards the stage as applause erupted from the audience. "Gotta run. I need to sign off the show."

He picked up his microphone and ran towards the stage, dodging the performers as they ran off.

Tristan introduced the cast members as he ran from the wings to center stage. They took a bow and ran back to the dressing rooms. Olivia head the applause crescendo when Tristan introduced the two lead singers.

Rachel, her brow furrowed, limped up to Olivia. "Is Kate alright?"

Olivia shook her head. "It's not good. She either has a bad sprain or she might even have broken it, according to Dr. Kohli."

"Oh no, that's so awful. A broken foot or ankle is serious business for a dancer. She's only been the dance captain for a week."

Mary stood quietly in front of Olivia.

"Oh, Mary. Sorry. I didn't mean to block your spot at the makeup table." Olivia moved to the side of the dressing room.

"It's fine." Mary sat down in front of the mirror, pulled out a makeup wipe, and began taking off her stage makeup.

"Rachel, are you okay?" Sara put her foot on her chair and unbuckled her shoe.

Rachel shrugged.

Tristan knocked on the dressing room door. "Rachel, I need you to go down to B deck and have Dr. Kohli check you over. That was a pretty serious fall."

Rachel shrugged. "I'm sure I'm fine; but whatever you say, boss." She sat down and unbuckled her shoe. The strap dug into her skin.

Hayley sat next to Rachel and looked at her foot. "Rach, your foot looks swollen."

"It's fine." Rachel rotated her ankle and bit her lip. "Nothing a little rest won't fix."

"Tristan is right to have Dr. Kohli check you out. You don't want to do more damage to it if something is wrong." Hayley released the clips that held her feathered headpiece. She pulled it off and took off the stocking wig cap underneath. She shook her copper hair out. "Do you want Olivia and me to walk you down?"

Olivia nodded in agreement.

Mary offered. "Sara and I can walk Rachel down."

Rachel stood up and winced. "That's okay, Mary. You guys need to get your costumes put away. Can you handle mine and Kate's, too? Thanks, Hayley. I'll take you up on your offer to walk down with me."

Olivia and Hayley each gave Rachel an arm to balance on and trudged toward the crew elevators.

"Do you want me to call for a wheelchair?"

Rachel shook her head. "No, I'll be fine. I finished the show. I can walk to the doctor's office."

"Yeah, but you had all that adrenaline on stage to push you through." Hayley slowed her step.

"True, but I am really okay."

The three girls hobbled into Dr. Kohli's waiting room. The door to the exam room was closed. They sat down in the hard waiting room chairs.

"I hope my foot isn't seriously hurt. I don't want to miss shows. Do you think they will send me home?"

Hayley squeezed Rachel's hand. "I hope not."

"Not only for me, but the cast has been through so much change with Candi leaving and then Kate coming to take her place." Rachel swallowed. "Sorry, Olivia. I forgot about Candi and Peter."

"Don't apologize. It isn't your fault that my boyfriend cheated with Candi. The fault lies squarely on Peter."

Hayley tilted her head. "And Candi."

Olivia shrugged. "Peter is the one who cheated on me. No one made him do that. Not even Candi."

"Candi was dating Lorenzo, the head waiter, last I heard."

"Then Lorenzo has a right to be angry with her. We can't change what happened, anyway." Olivia bit her lip. "I hope it is only something minor, Rachel."

The doorknob turned, and Alex backed out of the exam room, pulling Kate's wheelchair. He turned the wheelchair towards Rachel. Kate's elevated lower leg and foot were wrapped in white bandages. "I'm going to have to talk to you so I can fill out an accident report."

Rachel nodded.

Kate looked up. "Are you hurt, too, Rach?"

"I guess we'll see what Dr. Kohli says. What's up with your foot?" Rachel asked.

"It's not good." Kate's voice quavered. "It's broken."

Rachel caught her breath. "Kate, that's awful. I'm so sorry."

"Dr. Kohli said I'll probably need to be in a cast for 8 weeks. He's sending me home to my folks when we reach Barbados tomorrow."

"Oh, no!" Olivia squeezed Kate's hand. "Do you need me to help you pack?"

Kate nodded. "That would be wonderful. Thank you."

"I'll come by your cabin later."

"Thanks."

Dr. Kohli's nurse came up and wheeled Kate to the back of the infirmary.

"I hope he doesn't send me home." Rachel sighed. She limped through the exam room's open door.

Alex sat down in the chair next to Olivia. "For once, I'm going to have to write an incident report that doesn't involve you."

Olivia raised her eyebrow. "Very funny, Alex."

"I wasn't joking." The corner of Alex's mouth twitched. "Although since you are here, maybe I made an assumption that I shouldn't have. You aren't involved in Kate and Rachel slipping on the stairs, are you?"

"Of course not." Olivia's blue eyes flashed. "How could you even ask me a thing like that?"

"Olivia, I was just kidding you."

Olivia crossed her arms and tilted her head to the side. "Right."

Alex stood up and looked over his shoulder, and grinned at Olivia on his way out of the infirmary. "Give my best to Chico. Tell him I said he's the coolest bird I ever met."

"I'll pass your kind words on to Chico when I get back to my cabin."

Hayley elbowed Olivia. "I think he was flirting with you." Hayley's eyes widened. "Did you flirt back? Did I just see Olivia Morgan flirting? If so, we need to work on your flirting skills."

Olivia shook her head. "I wasn't flirting. Not every conversation between a man and a woman is flirting, Haley. Besides, I said I was done with men. I am obviously not good at picking men. The only good choice I've made with a male was adopting Chico."

"Thanks for helping me pack. I could hardly get this stupid chair through the door. There are only two feet of floor in this cabin. There is no way I could have gotten my stuff packed."

"I'm happy to help." Olivia pushed the wheelchair out into the hall and pulled Kate's suitcase out from under her bunk. "Which closet is yours?"

"The one on the left." Kate grimaced as she shifted her leg.

"Do you need a pillow under your foot?" Olivia gently lifted Kate's leg and slid a pillow under.

"That helps, thanks." Tears welled up in Kate's eyes. "I'm sorry. I am being such a baby."

"Don't be sorry! You are in pain."

"The pain isn't the worst part. I have wanted to be the dance captain in the cast ever since I started on ships. I finally get that job and I get hurt. The X-ray was terrible. I don't know if I'll ever be able to dance again, let alone be the dance captain. All I have ever wanted to do was dance. I don't know what I'll do if I can't dance again."

Olivia pulled the desk chair next to Kate and sat down. She took Kate's hand in hers and rubbed it. "Oh, sweetie. I am so sorry."

Kate squeezed Olivia's hand. "I sound so whiney."

"No! You have every right to feel that way. This is a horrible thing that happened to you. When Peter left, I didn't know what I would do. Other than some temp jobs between contracts, I have just worked on ships for the past few years. I thought about going back home, but I don't know what I would do there. Not the same as what you are going through, but I know how awful it is when your life gets turned upside down. I still don't know if I am going to make the show work."Olivia sighed. "If I get fired, I don't even know what I would want to do."

"Unfortunately, I know exactly what I will do if I can't dance again."

"Unfortunately?"

"Yeah, my parents own a restaurant. My brothers and sister work for them. They have been pushing for years for me to work for them in the family business."

"And you don't want to do that?"

"No! My entire childhood was spent at the restaurant. My parents were gone nights and every weekend. I don't want that life. I want to see the world and have freedom. It's my dream to work on cruise ships."

"Ship life is pretty addictive."

"It is."

Olivia patted Kate's hand. "There's no point in worrying about it now. Dr. Kohli didn't say you wouldn't dance again, did he?"

Kate shook her head.

"Alright then. Let's not buy trouble. Your job is to go home, rest and heal and do your physical therapy and come back as soon as your foot is strong enough."

Kate smiled. "You're right. I always go to the worst-case scenario. I'm a glass half empty person, I guess."

Olivia shrugged. "No, you aren't. It sounds like you know who you are and what you want. That is a wonderful way to go through life. I have just followed what Peter wanted and never really thought about what I wanted. For the first time in my life, I'm trying to figure out what would make me happy."

"I watched your show with Hayley. You did great."

"It went better than I feared, that's for sure. But I couldn't have pulled it off without Hayley."

The cabin door opened.

"Oh, I didn't know you were here." Mary threw her bag on her bunk.

"Hey. I'm helping Kate pack."

Mary glanced at the empty suitcase in front of Olivia's feet.

"I guess I need to get working on it." Olivia laughed.

"I can pack for her." Mary offered.

"Can you get her stuff from the bathroom?"

"Sure."

Olivia reached into the closet and pulled out a pile of clothes. She folded them and put them in the suitcase. Mary brought out Kate's toiletries and handed them to Olivia. Olivia put them in a plastic bag and tucked them in the suitcase.

Mary sat crossed-legged on her bunk and opened her dance bag. Mary pulled out her tap shoes and used a cloth soaked in cleaner to get scuff marks off of them.

"Which drawers are yours, Kate?"

"The top two."

Olivia pulled the top drawer open and grabbed the clothes inside. She folded them and put them in the suitcase.

"Do you want me to clean and polish your tap shoes, Kate?"

Kate cocked her head. "Gosh, I don't know where they are. Did I leave them in the dressing room or in Dr. Kohli's office?"

Olivia shook her head. "I can't remember when you took them off."

Mary stood up. "I'll go find them and bring them back."

"Thanks, Mary. I appreciate it. You are both such good friends. Thanks for helping me."

"You'd do the same for us." Olivia opened up the next drawer and started putting the items in Kate's bag. "Is Joseph your cabin steward?"

Kate nodded.

"I'll talk to him and get him to take your bag down to the gangway in the morning for you." Olivia looked around the tiny cabin. "Is there anything else you need me to pack?"

Kate thought for a second and then shook her head. "I think that is it."

Olivia leaned over and gave Kate a hug. "If you need anything, call me, okay? I'll see you when you get back."

"If I can come back."

O livia's flip-flops squeaked as she and Hayley walked up the pier towards their ship. Olivia breathed in the sweet smell of molasses from the rum distillery. She transferred her beach bag from her left shoulder to her right. "What a perfect day!"

"Truly, it is." Hayley raised her face to the sun and soaked up the warmth. Speckles of light filtered through her straw hat and radiated across her face. "...best job in the entire world."

Olivia smiled. "Most days, yes. It really is. I feel so badly for Kate. She's scared she won't heal enough to come back and dance."

"It's a dancer's worst nightmare to have an injury like hers. I'm heartbroken for her. It just goes to show you how precious this is." Hayley gestured at the ocean and their ship.

"Sample, pretty ladies?" In the terminal, a woman at a booth offered them small shot glasses of rum.

"Why not?" Hayley giggled, took the cups, and handed one to Olivia. They drank down the rum.

"Mmm." Olivia exhaled.

"We'll let the passengers know that you have excellent rum."

"Thank you, ma'am." She took their empty cups and threw them in her trash can.

"Where else can you get samples of rum on your way to work?"

"That is an awesome benefit of working on a cruise ship." Olivia licked her lips. "Thank you for stepping in and doing my show with me when Peter left. If you hadn't, I wouldn't have been able to keep this job."

"My pleasure. I'm having a blast doing the show with you and Chico. Any idea what you are going to add to the show so you can give Peter his half?"

Olivia pinched the bridge of her nose. "I was up for hours last night going over the show, the props, what I think we might be able to pull off. I'm really nervous we won't have enough material."

"Didn't mean to stress you out. We'll figure it out. After seeing how well the sections with Chico and I went, I'm not worried. The audience ate up his cute little self belting out show tunes. I can sing show tunes for hours. Chico and I can fill in wherever you need. We'll be fine."

Olivia sighed. "I sure hope so. We were struggling to get enough time last week and now we have to replace half of what we did."

"Not really. You told Peter you would give him half of the show. But there were already tricks that you didn't use last week because you didn't know how to do them. We can put all of that directly into the pile to give to Peter."

Olivia shrugged. "That's true. That makes me feel a little better."

Tristan was standing at the end of the crew gangway, talking with a redheaded woman.

Hayley slowed her step. "Oh, no."

Olivia turned and looked at Hayley. "Are you okay?"

"Yeah, but I'm not sure if you are going to be okay in a minute."

"What? Why?"

Hayley nodded towards Tristan. "Tristan is talking to Candi."

Olivia stopped walking. She took a deep breath and let it out in a rush.

"I bet Tristan had her fly out to replace Kate."

"Makes sense. Yuck. I really don't want to deal with her."

Tristan caught sight of them and gestured for them to come over.

"Ugh." Olivia pulled her straw hat down lower on her head.

"I'll go over and talk to them. You can just wave and go on the ship."

"No, I'll go with you." Olivia shifted her hat further back on her head. "I will not hide from her. I have nothing to be embarrassed about."

"Olivia, Hayley. Glad I caught you." Tristan smiled at Hayley. "I called Candi last night, and she agreed to fly out today and rejoin the ship. We're lucky she didn't have another contract. Isn't that wonderful?"

Olivia's eyes darted from Tristan to Candi. Candi tucked her hair behind her ear, looked at Olivia, and smirked.

Hayley gave a tight smile. "Yeah, wonderful."

"Can you and Candi catch up with Fernando and set up a run-through before the show tomorrow night?"

"Of course."

Tristan grinned at Hayley. He gestured for them to enter the ship. Candi picked up her luggage and handed her carry-on to Olivia. She sashayed up the gangway, tossing her red hair as she walked.

Olivia's face flushed. Hayley grabbed the carry-on out of Olivia's hand. "I've got it. Go feed Chico and I'll come to grab you for dinner. Okay?"

Olivia nodded. She held back as the trio walked up the gangway, flashed their IDs at security, and entered the ship. Olivia fished her ID out of her pocket, took a deep breath, and looked up at the ship. Her excitement about being on the ship had faded.

Olivia flashed her ID to security and headed to her cabin.

Chico greeted her when she opened her cabin door and danced back and forth on his perch. He wiggled his wings, begging her to pick him up.

"Chico, let me put away my stuff. Then I'll pick you up."

"Patooey."

"Have a little patience, bird."

Olivia put her bag in her closet, washed the sunblock off her face, and stood in front of Chico's cage. "What do you say, Mister?"

"Up!"

"Close enough." Olivia opened his cage door and reached in. "Up."

Chico stepped onto her hand. She brought him up to her chest, and he leaned against her while she pet him under his wing. He purred like a cat.

"You silly bird." Olivia sighed. "You won't believe who I just ran into?"

Chico tilted his head.

"Candi. That's who."

"Treat!"

"No, not that kind of candy. Although I get the impression that this Candi fancies herself quite the treat." Olivia shook her head. "If Peter had to cheat on me, the very least he could have done was have better taste."

"Mmmm."

"You obviously can't think of anything but food, can you, birdie?" Olivia pulled out the drawer with Chico's snacks and popped a few almonds in the dish on top of his cage, and put him on his perch. "Down."

Chico happily stepped onto his perch and picked up an almond with his foot.

He felt along the seam with his beak and then cracked it open. He dropped the shell and gleefully ate the almond. "Mmmm. Nut!"

"Glad you're happy. I wish all it took to make me happy was an almond."

Hayley knocked on the door and came in. "Sorry about that."

Olivia shrugged. "It is what it is. It's only for a few weeks until Kate comes back, right? I can deal with her for that long."

"Actually, Tristan said that he offered Candi a six-month contract, and she agreed to stay. When Kate heals up, she'll join one of the other production show casts that is just starting their contract. He said that they don't know how long it'll take Kate to get better and he didn't want to have to change lead dancers again if Kate wasn't ready to join the ship in time."

Olivia wrinkled her nose. "Poor Kate."

"I'm sorry you are stuck with Candi for your entire contract."

"Obviously, I don't like what she and Peter did. But I'm not giving her the satisfaction of being upset with her."

"Sounds like a good plan." Hayley turned to Chico and sang a few notes.

Chico cocked his head and continued to eat his almond.

Olivia laughed. "Sorry, I should have held off on giving him a snack until after you got here. Once he has an almond, he has zero interest in anything else."

"Apparently, he works for treats and not out of the pure love for performing."

"Let's be honest. That's why we all work, right?"

Hayley laughed and tossed her hair. "Speak for yourself. I'm an artist."

Olivia opened up her desk drawer and pulled out a small chocolate bar. She handed it to Hayley.

Hayley unwrapped it and popped a piece in her mouth. "An artist who loves treats."

"Treat!"

"That's right, Chico. Treat! Now that I have had my desert, are you ready to go to dinner?" Hayley licked the chocolate off of her fingers.

"Yes, I'm starving. All that sun, sand, and saltwater today made me hungry. Lido Buffet or Officer's mess?"

"Lido?"

"Perfect."

Olivia and Hayley grabbed their trays and picked out their food. Olivia looked for an open table.

Fernando raised his hand and waved for them to come join him at his table.

Olivia nodded and walked toward him. A woman with bright red hair sat next to Fernando. It was too late to veer away and find another table. She took a deep breath and attempted to put on a pleasant face.

Olivia sat down in the open seat next to Mary.

Hayley sat between Candi and Sara. "Hey! How are you all doing?"

"Fabulous! Wonderful to be back as the dance captain of our little company."

Mary slouched down over her plate and picked at her food. Sara rolled her eyes as she took a bite of her salad.

"Hayley, I'm so glad we ran into you." Fernando put his fork down and leaned in towards Hayley. "With Candi back and Rachel on medical leave for the next show, we need to do a quick blocking run-through of tomorrow night's show. It's shouldn't take long. After all, Candi knows all the dances. We just need to adjust them for being down one dancer."

"Of course. When were you thinking?"

Fernando looked at Candi. "What works for you?"

"I'm exhausted from the past few days." Candi shrugged one shoulder and looked at Olivia. "I need my beauty rest tonight. How about ten tomorrow morning?"

Mary looked up. "I'm supposed to go snorkeling tomorrow morning when we get into port."

"Surely you can do that another day, can't you?" Candi finished her glass of wine.

Fernando pulled a schedule out of his pocket and read through it. "Ten works for me. The theatre will be empty, so that's a perfect time. I've got to run. I need to get to the comedian's sound check. See you all in the morning." He picked up his tray and headed out.

Candi yawned. "While I'd love to say and chat, I need to unpack."

"Don't let us keep you." Hayley smiled at Candi. "I'm sure you must be exhausted with all you've been up to this week."

Candi paused, cocked her head, and then picked up her tray and left. She turned her head to see if they were watching her walk away.

"Ugh." Olivia rolled her eyes. She covered her mouth with her hand. "Sorry. Shouldn't have said that out loud."

Sara shrugged. "You're fine. Don't worry about it."

"Hayley, maybe after your run-through, you and I can go through the illusion cases and see what we have that we know we can use and what we need to put on the manifest to get offloaded for Peter."

"That sounds like a good idea. We probably won't have time to get off the ship after the run-through anyway since it is a tender port. Might as well just stay on the ship and work."

Mary sighed.

"I don't want to ruin your day, Hayley. If you want to get off the ship, I can go through the cases myself."

"No! I'm happy to go through them with you. It'll be good for me to see what the options are. Plus, I can help you with the heavy stuff."

"Places!" Fernando signaled to Nigel to start the click track.

Olivia sat crossed-legged on one of her cases in the stage left wing. Chico perched on her leg and bobbed up and down to the music.

Olivia had hoped that the cast would be gone by the time she got to the theatre. The run-through was taking longer than Hayley had expected.

Olivia opened up one of the close-up magic cases and laid out the props.

She sorted them into three sections. Props she knew how to use and was planning to keep, ones that she did not know how to perform and would give to Peter, and one pile of things that she thought she could learn, but wanted to go over with Hayley for her thoughts.

The music halted. Fernando gestured for Candi to come off stage. She pushed down the seat and sat next to him in the front row.

The cast groaned. Mary sunk down onto the stage and put her head in her hands.

"Sorry I told you to come up at 11, Liv. I really thought we'd be done by now."

Hayley picked up Chico and gave him a kiss.

"Mwah!" Chico made a kissing noise.

"Fernando has to keep stopping the rehearsal because Candi won't stay in formation. She keeps cutting in front of Mary and Sara. She almost knocked into me, trying to get upfront. Candi is insufferable."

"I'm sorry your rehearsal isn't going well, but Chico and I have kept ourselves busy." Olivia gestured towards the props laid out on the trunk lid.

"Interesting. I don't know what most of that is. Do you?"

"Oh yes. I know what all of it is. I just don't know how to use this stuff over here." Olivia gestured towards the pile she'd put aside for Peter. "I have performed the stuff in this pile before, so I'm keeping that. It's this pile here that I thought you and I could go over so I could get your opinion."

"Chico, Chico, Chico!" Chico danced back and forth.

"Sorry, I meant to say you, me, and Chico. He wants to be a part of the decision-making process, apparently."

Candi's shout drew their attention. She had her hands on her hips. Her taps ricocheted off the floor as she stomped her silver-shoed foot.

Fernando clenched his jaw. He pursed his lips in a tight line.

Hayley shook her head. "I do not know how he puts up with her. She's even worse than she was in her last contract."

Nigel left the sound booth and walked down next to Candi. He put his hand on her shoulder and tried to calm her.

"Get your hands off of me." Candi's shrill voice cut through the theatre.

"Poor Nigel. Why do guys fawn all over her? I don't get it. She's so nasty." Hayley looked at Olivia and wrinkled her nose. "Sorry. I wasn't thinking."

Olivia shrugged. "It's okay. I don't get it either."

"Peter was an idiot to leave you for her."

"She's pretty." Olivia shrugged.

"Not as pretty as you are, and not as pretty as she thinks she is. That's for sure."

"She's talented."

"Yes, but Mary and Sara are both better technically." "

"I wish Tristan had just promoted either of them instead of bringing Candi back."

"Mary just doesn't have star power like Candi does. She's too quiet. Sara is so young. She's not ready to be dance captain yet."

Fernando walked onstage. "Alright. I think we're done for the day. Candi wants to be on Hayley's stage right side. Mary, you're going to be in the back row with Sara."

Mary glared at Candi as Candi strutted back to the dressing room. Candi raised her chin and pointedly ignored Hayley and Olivia as she walked by.

"So Fernando caved and let her have her way. It's ridiculous." Hayley shook her head. "Mary ends up being right behind me through the routine. She might as well take the night off since no one can see her."

"Uh oh!" Chico cocked his head.

Mary slowly stood up and walked back to the dressing room with the rest of the cast.

"Show me what you've got in that third pile."

Olivia pulled out the props and talked Haley through what each one was supposed to do. Hayley had a couple of good ideas about how they could use a couple in the show. The rest they added to Peter's pile.

"Help me move the stairs so we can get back to the illusion cases."

Hayley and Olivia unlocked the castors and pushed the stairs on stage. Olivia slipped on the floor, and Hayley caught her before she fell. "Oh! What the heck?"

There was a wet spot on the stage floor. Olivia got a paper towel from the dressing room and bent down to clean it up.

"I think it's oil or grease. Look at this." Olivia held up the stained paper towel. She walked under the stairs and looked up. "Do you think the stairs are leaking oil? Maybe that's why Kate fell."

"Could be. Maybe the stage crew had greased something on the staircase and dripped some. We'll have to let Fernando know, so it doesn't happen again."

Olivia covered her mouth with her hand. "Oh, my! Do you think someone intentionally put oil on the stairs?"

"Livvy, you know how much I love you, but you are losing it. I know the last cruise was enough to make anyone paranoid, but I'm sure it was just a mistake by the stage crew."

"You're right." Olivia covered her eyes with her hand. "Sorry for being so dramatic."

Olivia and Hayley pulled out the illusion cases and opened them up.

Olivia lifted the lid on the substitution trunk. "This one might work. We didn't have time for me to teach it to you last week since we had so much else to learn, but I think we should be able to make it work. Help me lift it out of its case."

"You have a trunk stored inside another trunk?" Hayley cocked her head.

Olivia laughed. "I know that looks ridiculous, but it's in a travel case, so it doesn't get broken when it's shipped. The cruise lines send everything cargo. The illusions need to be protected."

"Makes sense." Hayley grabbed the handle of the substitution trunk and they lifted it out of the case. "Wow! That is heavy."

"Yep. Setting up the show, performing it, and then tearing it down is a good way to stay in shape. It's a workout just getting all the illusions set up."

"Seriously. I might need to add a weight workout to my yoga!"

They rolled the trunk to center stage and locked the castors. Olivia put a hoop with a fabric curtain around the trunk and dropped it to the stage floor. She hooked the edge of the hoop onto the edge of the trunk. "Do you want to start out in the trunk or on top of it?"

Hayley made a questioning face. "On top, I guess."

"It'll be fun, I promise. Let me show you what it looks like." Olivia stood on top of the trunk and grabbed the hoop. She lifted the hoop to her waist and looked at Hayley. "Ready?"

Olivia raised the hoop, and it dropped to the floor.

She was gone.

"Okay. I've seen you and Peter perform that before, but never this close. How the heck did you do that?"

Olivia's muffled voice came from inside the trunk. "Let me out so I can show you."

Hayley laughed. "Fair enough." She opened the lock on the front of the trunk and lifted the lid. Olivia popped up.

"Seriously. How did you do that?" Hayley shook her head. "I want to know, but I also don't want to know. You know what I mean?"

"I do. But knowing how the tricks work is fun, too. It becomes a competition with yourself to do it better and cleaner than you did it the time before. Come over here so I can show you what you need to know."

Hayley walked hesitantly towards the trunk.

"It won't bite you."

"It might. You never know."

"This time, I'm going to do the trick, but without the hoop and curtain, so you can see what I do."

"I'm ready."

Olivia climbed on top of the trunk. She pretended to lift the hoop to her waist, nodded at Hayley, and then pretended to throw the hoop in the air. She was gone in a split second.

"Whoa, that was so fast!"

"That's kind of the point. Let me out, please."

Hayley opened the trunk lid. "I'm really impressed. That is so cool."

Olivia stepped out of the trunk. "Your turn!"

"Oh, boy." Hayley climbed up on top of the trunk. "It feels higher than I thought it would be. Maybe I picked the wrong part of the trick."

"You're only three feet off the ground. It probably just feels higher because the stage is elevated."

"Three feet is a lot. You know how I feel about heights." Hayley looked down at the stage floor.

"Don't look down. Focus on the sound and light board at the back of the auditorium. We'll try it a couple of times like this and then we can trade if it doesn't work for you."

"Okay. I'll give it my best shot."

They ran the trick twice.

Olivia let her out of the trunk.

"Ok, the drop isn't as bad as I feared, but the landing is rough."

"Yes. When we first got this trick, I had to wear double layers of tights to cover the bruises on my legs."

"Sure! Now you tell me."

"Do you want to switch, Hayley? I don't mind. It is good if we both know how to do the trick both ways in case something happens but I'm fine with being outside."

Hayley looked at the trunk. "No. If you can do it, I want to do it, too."

"That's the spirit." Olivia put her arm around Hayley and gave her some hints on how to land in a way that wouldn't hurt. "Are you ready to add the hoop and the handcuffs?"

"Handcuffs?" Hayley's eyes widened.

"Yes, handcuffs. When I'm in the trick in the beginning, I'm wearing them. When we switch positions and you're in the trunk, you are wearing them."

"Goodness. I'm glad we started rehearsing this today. It's way more involved than I thought it would be. Part of me thought there was like a button or something."

Olivia laughed. "No, no button."

"So, what am I going to be wearing? Maybe seeing my pretty costume will be motivating. Tell me it is sparkly. You know how I love sequins."

"Let's go into the dressing room and I'll show you a couple of options. Then I need to feed Chico. I'm sure he's ready for his lunch."

"He's not the only one."

"How about we do two more run-throughs and then go to lunch? I'll grab some goodies for Chico."

"Deal!"

6

Olivia couldn't tell if it was the tropical sun on her face, or the irritation she felt that was making her cheeks flush.

"Careful, you might burn a hole in the back of Candi's head, glaring at her like that."

"I don't want to give her any attention. It's just... that fake laugh is so irritating." Olivia rolled her eyes. "Who wears heels on a walking tour of a botanical garden?"

"They're sandals with a low heel, but probably not the most practical walking shoe. They show off her dancer's legs, though." Haley sighed. "She seems to have Nigel and Tristan enthralled."

Olivia shook her head. "Tristan is just being polite to her, I'm sure."

Haley shrugged. "Tristan can do whatever he wants and flirt with whomever he chooses. It's not my business."

"Right." Olivia smiled.

"It's just that we know what kind of person she is. You know better than anyone."

"That's true. But the difference is that Tristan is a good guy and Peter, apparently, is not. Tristan can't take his eyes off of you."

Hayley looked at Tristan. He glanced over his shoulder, caught her eye, and grinned.

"See?"

Hayley smiled. "Maybe you're right. I guess I shouldn't be complaining that she's here. I'm sure you're not thrilled Nigel invited her to come along."

"I've been so looking forward to this tour that I will not let Candi stop me from enjoying it. I've never seen a Jaco or Sisserou parrot in person before, only pictures of them in books. To get to see them up close is so exciting." Olivia's face lit up, and she sighed. "I know I get to see Chico every day, so seeing another Amazon parrot shouldn't be this exciting. But I can't wait. I'm sorry for going on a tangent."

"Livy, don't apologize for being excited. I think it is awesome that we get to see them, too. I adore Chico. It'll be fun to see his cousins."

"I didn't want to miss out on the chance to see them just because Candi was coming on the tour. I didn't do anything wrong, so why should I avoid her?"

"No, you didn't do anything wrong. She is the one that should be embarrassed to be around you."

"Oh Tristan, you're so witty." Candi giggled and rubbed Tristan's arm. She looked back at Olivia and Hayley, making sure they were paying attention.

Hayley rolled her eyes. "She sure lays it on thick."

"Look at Nigel." Olivia gestured towards him. "He can't take his eyes off of her. He looks miserable that she's flirting with Tristan."

"He looks like a puppy dog that got kicked. I truly don't understand what guys see in her." Hayley shrugged. "She's pretty, but everything about her is fake."

"Well, whatever she has going on is working for her."

The group walked through the entrance to the botanical garden and stepped over the concrete curb onto the grass to avoid walking in the road.

"It's such a pretty orange flower." Olivia cupped a flower in her hand and sniffed it. "It doesn't look real."

Hayley read a plaque on the tree. "Maybe if I had taken Latin in school, this would make more sense."

They passed a gardener raking up the leaves under the trees.

Their tour guide walked them to a shady spot under the canopy of a tree. "Can you guess what this tree is called?"

The group looked up at the tree. Large brown fruit hung from the branches above their heads.

Nigel guessed. "Potato tree?"

Candi rolled her eyes and shook her head at his guess.

Nigel's shoulders sank.

"Good guess." The tour guide nodded his approval. "It's actually called the Sausage tree."

Rumbles of laughter spread throughout the group.

Mary nudged Nigel. "You were close."

Nigel shrugged his shoulders.

Olivia tried to replicate the chirping of the little brown and yellow birds that filled a nearby bush. "It's easier to talk to Chico. He understands what I'm saying. At least most of the time."

"Our gardens have been here since the 1930s. In 1979, a fierce hurricane hit our island. You can still see some of the damage that was done." The tour guide gestured towards a school bus that was crushed under a tree. "Thankfully, no one was inside the bus at the time the baobab tree fell on it."

Fernando stood in front of the bus and pretended that he was being squished. Olivia snapped his picture and laughed.

"Many of our plants have medicinal properties. There are also some that are toxic." The tour guide gestured towards a plant with small red berries. "This is the Solanum Bahamense. It is in the same family as poisonous plants like belladonna and mandrake. See the spikes on the leaves? You do not want to touch this plant."

Olivia stepped away from the plant.

"Have you ever done any magic tricks with poison?" Hayley asked.

"No. And I'm not going to start now."

The tour guide motioned for the group to stand in front of a banyan tree. "Here, hand me your camera and I will take a picture of your group." He put his hand out to Olivia. She opened the camera and handed him her phone.

"Mary! Over here! We're going to get a group picture taken."

Mary left the plant she was looking at and caught up to the group.

They crowded in next to each other, some holding the huge roots that hung down from the tree. Candi pushed herself to the front and center of the group. She nudged Mary out of the way and stood directly in front of Olivia.

The group shouted "Cheese" as the tour guide snapped their picture. He handed Olivia her phone.

"Now, for the most exciting part of our tour. Our conservation facility for our national parrots, the Jaco and the Sisserou. The Sisserou is our national bird and is on our flag. Both are native to our island."

The Sisserou's dark head bobbed up and down. He looked back at the group looking at him. Olivia got as close to the enclosure as she could. His bright orange eye followed her as she moved.

Hayley pointed at the parrot. "His colors aren't as bright as Chico's."

"No, he isn't as flashy as a double yellow Amazon, like Chico, but he is still beautiful. Look at the dark blue on the back of his neck and the rust color on his cheeks. Those orange eyes get your attention!"

"Sure do. I wonder if they like snacks as much as Chico?"

"I'm not sure anyone likes snacks as much as Chico."

The tour guide directed them to another enclosure.

"Oh, it's the Jaco!" Olivia's eyes lit up.

Two parrots with light blue heads sat on a high perch in a corner of the cage. The tour guide took out a peanut and held it up. One parrot made his way down the perch and plucked the peanut from the tour guide's hand. He held the peanut with his foot and split the shell with his beak.

"I guess that answers our question about snacks."

"He looks a lot like Chico, but with a blue face."

Olivia asked the tour guide a few questions about the parrots. The rest of their group wandered away, looking at the plants and birds.

Olivia caught up with Hayley. "What an amazing job he has. Can you imagine how much fun it would be to work with parrots all day? And get paid for it!"

"Olivia, isn't that what you do?"

Olivia laughed. "Sort of. It's not quite the same training Chico and doing the show, but you have a point."

"This is the conclusion of our tour. I am so glad you came to visit our garden today. Please tell guests on the ship about us and invite them to come and visit us. If you would like, there is one more attraction here in the garden." The tour guide gestured towards a set of steps. "Those steps lead up to a path that takes you to an overlook. You will see your ship from the summit. You are welcome to hike up there."

Tristan looked at his watch.

"Do you have time to do the hike?" Hayley bit her lip.

"I think I can make it work." Tristan gestured for Hayley to start up the stone steps.

Candi pushed past Nigel, Mary, and Sara. She raced to catch up to Tristan. "Tristan, wait for me. I'm coming, too!"

Nigel trudged behind her.

"Do you guys want to do the hike?" Fernando and Mary nodded. They followed the rest of the group up the steep steps. At the top of the steps, they turned left and walked along the dirt path. Birds chirped in the surrounding trees.

The sun beat down on Olivia. She had forgotten her straw hat. She wiped the sweat that was dripping into her eyes. "Wow, this path is steep!"

"Seriously. We're getting a workout today, aren't we?"

Fernando looked back at Mary. "Are you ok?"

Mary nodded and continued up the hill.

Olivia pushed on her side with her hand. Her breathing roared in her ears.

They turned another corner. Foliage shaded the stairs, bringing some relief from the sun.

Candi was sitting on a step, holding her shoe. The strap had rubbed her heal until it was pink. Nigel was fanning her with his map of the garden. "I said I was fine, Nigel."

Nigel stopped fanning her. He looked at the rest of the group and shrugged.

Olivia and Fernando passed her and continued up the steps.

The path narrowed and became rougher the higher up they hiked.

Hayley paused. She kicked a rock, and it skipped along the path and then over the side, bouncing down the side of the mountain until they couldn't hear it anymore. Hayley looked over the edge of the path. "I'm not sure this hike is for me."

Tristan moved over, putting Hayley on the inside of the path. "It's alright. I won't let you get close to the edge. I promise."

"I don't want you to get too close to the edge, either."

Tristan laughed. "Did you know that I've gone rock climbing before? This is nothing."

Hayley made a face and shivered. "I've gone snorkeling with sharks, but I will never go rock climbing."

"I know you are a brave, capable woman. I would be nervous around sharks."

Hayley smiled at Tristan and they continued up the path until they were out of sight.

Olivia looked back at the rest of the group. They were trudging up the steps a few yards back. Olivia stepped over the thick roots protruding out of the ground. She kept her eyes on the uneven path, carefully avoiding rocks. A little lizard ran across the path in front of her and then scuttled off into the underbrush.

"If I had known we were going to do a hike up a mountain, I would have worn my hiking boots instead of my sneakers." Olivia paused and lifted her foot up, pulling a stick out of her sneaker.

"At least you didn't wear fancy sandals like Candi." Fernando laughed.

Bamboo arched over the pathway, shading them from the sun.

Olivia spotted the ship through a break in the foliage. She pointed. "Look!"

Fernando stopped walking. "Wow. The ship looks so small from up here. What a beautiful view."

Screams from below broke the peace. Fernando and Olivia raced down the path, dodging rocks as they ran.

M ary and Nigel each held one of Candi's hands and were pulling her to a standing position.

"You oaf! You knocked me down." Candi brushed dirt off of her shorts.

Nigel shook his head and lifted his hands in the air. "No, I didn't knock you down. When I saw you wobble, I tried to grab you to keep you from falling. That's all."

Candi glared at him. She took off her sandals and walked up the path barefoot. She ignored Olivia and Fernando as she passed them.

Olivia shook her head and patted Nigel on the shoulder. "The view is worth the hike. Come on."

They reached the summit. Hayley and Tristan stood next to each other, gazing out at the view.

"Oh Livvy, isn't it beautiful? The turquoise blue of the Caribbean Sea never gets old."

"It is stunning. Worth the hike."

Candi leaned against a cannon on the overlook. "Ready to go down?"

"Oh, I want to enjoy the view for a bit," Hayley raised her hand to shield her eyes from the sun.

"I meant Tristan." Candi crossed her arms. "Don't you have to get back to the ship?"

"I do, but I have a few minutes before I have to leave."

"Fine. Mary, ready?"

"Actually..."

"Let's go."

Candi limped down the path with Mary in tow.

"Ouch!" Olivia rubbed her head.

"Sorry!"

"It's okay. That's why we're rehearsing. Things happen."

"There are just so many things going on at once. I zigged when I should have zagged." Hayley climbed out of the trunk. "Are you alright?"

"I'm fine. You just grazed me. Better that it happened in rehearsal than in front of the audience. The ship is rocking pretty good tonight. That makes it tricky to not hit each other on the way by. Let's do one more run-through tonight. If we can get through it without a mistake, do you want to grab something at the midnight buffet?"

"Sounds good. I'm starving. All of that hiking today and then rehearsing tonight. I have worked up an appetite."

Olivia pushed play on the music, and they ran through the trick.

"Much better. We need to get it up to speed, but you are getting there."

"That run-through felt better. At least I didn't bonk you on the head this time."

They put the trunk in its case and shoved it into the wings. They changed into their evening dresses and headed up to the buffet.

"Ah, they've put out the barf bags on the railings. They must expect some fun weather tonight."

"I thought it felt like it was getting worse."

They looked for a table. Tristan waved them over.

Hayley waved back. They walked towards his table. She slowed as she spotted Candi sitting next to him. "Do you want to sit somewhere else?"

"No, she doesn't bother me. Plus, Tristan wants you to sit with him."

Hayley sat on Tristan's other side.

"How did your rehearsal go?" Fernando asked.

"Not bad. A couple of bumps, but we're finding our rhythm. I think we'll have it ready by showtime."

"Excellent. Hey, tomorrow morning we need to do a run-through of tomorrow night's production show. Dr. Kohli hasn't cleared Rachel to perform, so we're going to need to re-block it."

Hayley wrinkled her nose. "Oh, no! Poor Rachel. I can be there. What time?"

"Would 10 work for you?"

"Sure."

"Let me know when you and Olivia get your show order done and we can go over the lights and sound."

"Sounds good, Fernando. I'll let you know as soon as we have it figured out."

Olivia smiled at Mary. "Did you enjoy the botanical garden today?"

Mary nodded. She took a bite of a canapé.

A waiter came around with a tray of hors d'oeuvres. He offered it first to Tristan and Candi.

"Is that tomato?" Candi asked.

The waiter nodded.

Candi shook her head. "Do you have the asparagus ones?"

He used his tongs to hand her a small asparagus quiche. Tristan held up his plate, and the waiter placed a couple of hors d'oeuvres on it. He made his way down the table until everyone had something.

The lights dimmed. Lorenzo entered the dining room, pushing a cart. He made his way to their table and glanced at Candi. Candi leaned into Tristan and whispered in his ear.

Lorenzo pulled his cart up next to Hayley. He picked up an orange and used a small knife to peel it in one long spiral. Hayley turned in her seat to watch him. He winked at her.

Hayley blushed.

Candi grabbed Tristan's arm and laughed. "Tristan, I've been meaning to ask you something.."

Tristan gave Candi a tight smile. He looked at Hayley and Olivia and rolled his eyes.

"Did you know that I've been working on my own solo show?" Candi glared at Olivia. "I got offered a contract on another cruise line, but it didn't work out."

Olivia shook her head and snorted.

Tristan patted Candi's hand and slid his arm out from underneath hers. "Let's talk about that tomorrow, okay?"

Candi crossed her arms and nodded. She slouched back in her chair.

Lorenzo poured brandy over the orange. The liquor followed the spiral of the peel and dripped into the pan of bubbling cherries on his cart. He flicked his lighter and held it up to the spiral of peel.

Flames traveled up the orange peel and enveloped the orange.

Hayley gasped. It was so close that she could feel the heat.

Their table clapped.

Candi stood up. "Please excuse me for a second. If the waiter comes back, I'd love another one of those darling little quiches." She walked past Lorenzo and jostled him.

The flaming orange shot out of his tongs and rolled across the carpet.

Lorenzo jumped back and grabbed a wet towel. He threw it over the orange, putting out the flames.

He glared at Candi.

"Oh goodness. Excuse me." Candi sashayed towards the ladies' room. She shook her long red hair and glanced over her shoulder at Lorenzo.

Their waiter rushed over and put his tray of hors d'oeuvres down at Candi's empty spot. He picked the towel and orange off the ground and carried them into the kitchen.

Sara picked a couple of canapés off the tray and put them on her plate. She selected a quiche and put it on Candi's plate.

Lorenzo picked up another orange and began pealing it in a spiral. After setting the orange on fire, he used the tongs to squeeze the juice into the pan of sautéed cherries.

Everyone clapped as the pan of cherries caught on fire. Lorenzo tossed the flaming cherries in the pan, and the flames dissipated. He put it back on the burner and plated a scoop of ice cream. Lorenzo scooped some cherries and poured them over the ice cream. He ladled up some of the sauce and poured it over the desert, then handed it to Hayley. He made his way around the table, handing each person a plate.

Their waiter came back and picked up his tray.

Mary took two servings of cherries jubilee and put one at Candi's spot.

Candi strutted out of the ladies' room. "Mmm, these little quiches are scrumptious. Thank you for getting it and the cherries jubilee for me, Tristan."

"Actually, Sara and Mary got them for you."

"Oh." Candi finished the quiche and pushed her plate away. She pulled the cherries jubilee into its place. She picked up her spoon and scooped up some cherries and ice cream and took a bite.

Lorenzo wheeled his cart across the dining room to another table.

Candi scowled.

Tristan turned to Hayley. "Thank goodness it's quiet in here tonight. If it had been a busy night, we would have had a panic that the ship was going to catch on fire."

"Nothing like a rough sea to empty out the midnight buffet."

"The Captain said we could have 30 to 40-foot surges tonight." Tristan took a bite of his dessert.

"Olivia and I noted that the barf bags were out. Figured that wasn't a great sign."

"We should be out of it by morning."

"That's good news." Hayley took another bite of her cherries.

"Tristan, I heard the most interesting thing the other day." Candi touched his hand. Tristan pulled his hand back and picked up his spoon.

Candi took another bite of her dessert. Her cheeks flushed pink. She reached up and rubbed her throat.

Candi reached for her glass of water. "Oh my, I think the rough sea is getting to me."

She picked up her napkin and wiped her forehead. "I'm not feeling well. Tristan, I think I need to go to my cabin. Could you walk me?"

Tristan put his spoon down. "Sure." Tristan's shoulders sank. He stood up and touched Hayley's shoulder.

She looked up at him.

"I'll see you in the morning?"

Hayley nodded.

He squeezed her shoulder and then gave Candi his arm.

Nigel watched Candi walk out. He stood up. "I'm hosting pool games in the morning, so I think I'm going to head to bed."

"Me too." Mary walked towards Nigel.

Fernando stood up and pushed in his chair. "Ladies. I'll see you at 10 tomorrow."

Sara followed him.

"Candi sure is something, isn't she?" Hayley scraped the last bit of sauce off her plate and licked her spoon. "Can you imagine faking being seasick to get a guy to take you to your cabin?"

"Tristan looked annoyed with her. I'm sure you don't have anything to worry about."

"I'm not worried about Tristan. Why would I be? He's just my boss."

"I can see that you guys like each other. I think it's great. He's a really nice guy."

"You really think he likes me?"

"Hayley, he can't take his eyes off of you. You are stunning. Did you notice Lorenzo flirting with you?"

"He was probably just trying to make Candi jealous since she dumped him for Peter."

"Well, if he was trying to make her jealous, it looked like it worked. I can't believe she knocked the flaming orange out of his hands."

"Places!" Fernando clapped his hands and the cast took their places on stage. "We're already running late. We have to be out of the theatre by 11:30 for Bingo."

Fernando looked at the cast lined up on stage. "Still no Candi? Has anyone seen Candi this morning?"

Everyone shook their heads no.

"This is ridiculous." Fernando slammed his clipboard down.

Mary raised her hand. "Do you want me to call her cabin?"

Fernando nodded. "That would be great."

Mary stood up and ran back into the dressing room. She returned a minute later. "She didn't answer. Do you want me to go looking for her?"

"No." Fernando looked at his watch. "She was supposed to be here 20 minutes ago. Mary, I'm going to put you in the lead position. Candi will have to dance behind you tonight."

Mary bounced up to Hayley's side and grinned.

Chico whistled along as Hayley sang. He bobbed his head up and down in time to the music.

"Bluebirds fly……"

"Birb! Birb!" Chico rocked back and forth.

"No, not birb, it's bird, with a d." Hayley explained to Chico.

"He knows how to say it. I think he just thinks it's funny to say it with a b." Olivia shrugged.

"Darn it, bird. This isn't a comedy act. We're supposed to be doing a very serious duet."

Chico chuckled. He started making clicking sounds and rocked back and forth.

"What is he doing?"

"I'm not sure. He's never made that sound before."

Hayley listened to Chico. She bobbed her head in time to the rhythm he clicked his tongue. "Oh, my goodness! He's tap dancing! I mean, he's making the sound our shoes make when we tap dance in that number on the stairs. Here, listen."

Hayley stood up and pretended to do the tap routine on the small bit of bare floor in front of Chico's cage. "Can you hear it?"

Chico bobbed his head up and down while making tap shoe sounds. He sang one last big note. "Laaaa!"

Olivia laughed. "I wouldn't have picked up on it if you hadn't said anything, but you are right. He must have learned it at rehearsal the other day."

"Maybe Chico and I can put together a routine where he and I tap dance together!"

"I love that idea. Oh! You could each do solos!"

"Love it!"

"Snack?" Chico tilted his head to one side and looked at Hayley and Olivia.

Olivia handed Sophie a hundred-dollar bill. "Can you make change for me? I need it for tips."

"Of course, mate. Ones and fives?"

"Fives and tens?"

"No worries." Sophie quickly counted out Olivia's change.

"Have you seen Candi this morning?" Hayley asked.

"No, I haven't. I'll let her know you are looking for her if I do."

"You don't have to do that. She never showed up at rehearsal, so I was just wondering if you had seen her." Hayley shrugged.

Olivia picked up her cash, put it in her wallet, and shoved it in her pocket. "Ready?"

Hayley nodded. They turned towards the elevators.

"Hayley!" Tristan came out of his office. "Hey, Olivia."

Hayley lit up. "Hi. How is your day going?"

"Could be better, could be worse. Tired after a late night last night."

Hayley's shoulders sank. "Oh, you and Candi had a late night?"

"Oh, oh no... nothing like that. After I dropped her at her cabin, I ended up in my office doing next week's activities schedule until late." Tristan shrugged. "So much fun."

Alex's office door shot open. He saw Tristan and hesitated mid-stride. He crossed the lobby and touched Tristan's shoulder. "Got a minute?"

Tristan nodded, and they stepped aside. Staticky voices came over the radio on Alex's hip. He picked it up, pushed the button on the side, and spoke into it. Alex leaned into Tristan and murmured in his ear.

Tristan reached his hands up and held his head. "Oh, no!"

Alex squeezed his shoulder. Alex nodded at Olivia and Hayley and ran down the stairs.

"I have to go."

Hayley touched Tristan's arm. "Are you okay? You don't look right."

"It's Candi."

"Candi?" Hayley rolled her eyes.

"Joseph found her dead when he went to service her cabin."

Hayley's hand flew to her mouth. "Oh no. That's awful."

"I have to go."

"Of course."

Tristan squeezed Hayley's hand and ran down the stairs.

Olivia raked her hands through her hair. "She said she wasn't feeling well last night, but I never dreamed she was that sick."

"Me either. I thought she was just trying to get Tristan to herself." Hayley shook her head. "I feel awful. When she didn't show up for rehearsal this morning, I was so angry. I thought such horrible things about her."

"She didn't give either of us any reason to like her."

"No. But she was so young." Tears streaked down Hayley's cheeks.

Olivia darted over to Sophie. "Do you have any tissues?"

Sophie looked at Hayley. "Here. Is she alright?"

"She'll be fine. It's Candi. Tristan just told us they found her dead in her cabin."

Sophie gasped. "The dancer? Oh, bless."

Olivia took the tissue to Hayley.

"I don't know why I'm crying." Hayley blotted her tears.

"Because you are a good person. I feel like an awful person. She is dead and I should be upset. I am in shock, but I can't help but be relieved that I don't have to deal with her for the rest of the contract."

"I doubt anyone would blame you for not being broken up over her death after her cheating with Peter. You have every right to not be her biggest fan."

"It isn't just the cheating part. Frankly, knowing what I know now, she's welcome to Peter. Heck, she did me a favor. She was just so difficult."

"Very true."

Hayley wiped her tears and took a deep breath. "I've got to track down Fernando and tell him. The production show is in just a few hours. I don't want to sound cold, but at least we blocked the routines without Candi this morning, so we'll have the choreography right for tonight. With Rachel still not cleared to perform and Candi..." Hayley gulped. "With Candi gone, the cast is going to be pretty sparse tonight."

"I'll help you find Fernando. Should we check the theatre?"

Hayley headed towards the stairs. "Yes, let's look there first. He's probably getting the sets in place for tonight."

The red velvet stage curtains were closed, but they heard the scraping of props and the chatter of the crew coming from behind it. They climbed the stairs to the stage and pushed the heavy curtain aside. The crew looked up, saw it was them, and went back to work.

"Fernando?" Olivia gestured for him to come over. "Can we talk in the dressing room?"

"Of course." Fernando turned towards his crew. "I'll be back in five."

Olivia led them backstage. "Fernando, we have some bad news."

Fernando nodded. "Are you leaving the ship?"

"No! Why would you think that? Has someone said I was going to leave?"

Fernando shook his head. "No, I just couldn't think of what else would be bad news that you would come talk to me about."

Olivia exhaled. "It's Candi. We just heard that she's dead."

Fernando gasped and sat down in one of the makeup chairs. "Dead? What happened?"

"I don't know. We were with him when Alex told him, but we didn't hear any details. We don't know anything else. We just wanted you to know because this will obviously impact the show."

"I need to talk to Tristan about how he wants me to handle the show tonight. I'm going to need to tell the rest of the cast. The sooner the better. I don't want to hit them with it right before curtain time." Fernando shook his head. "With the way gossip spreads on a cruise ship, they might already know."

"Hayley and I will go find Tristan. We'll have him contact you, ok?"

Fernando nodded and walked over to his crew.

Olivia and Hayley took the elevator to Tristan's office. Hayley knocked gently on his door.

"Come in."

Hayley opened his door. Tristan was resting his head in his hands. He looked up at them when they walked in. His eyes were red and swollen.

"I feel so guilty. She told me she wasn't feeling well. I couldn't wait to dump her in her cabin and get away from her." Tristan shook his head. "I should have checked on her. Or called Dr. Kohli. I'm an awful person."

Hayley walked behind his desk and rubbed his back. "Tristan. You are not an awful person. You were a perfect gentleman. Heck, you left your dessert and walked her to her cabin. How could you know she was seriously sick?"

Tristan stood up and gave Hayley a hug. She hugged him back, holding him until he relaxed in her arms. Tristan pulled back and looked at Olivia. "I'm sorry."

Olivia shook her head. "Don't be sorry. It's an awful thing."

Hayley sat down next to Olivia. "Fernando asked us to find you. He needs to know what you want him to do about the production show cast. Do you want him to tell them?"

"It should probably come from me. I'll call an emergency staff meeting." Tristan picked up the phone. "Nigel, I need to see all the entertainment and cruise staff in the theatre in 30 minutes. Try to reach as many as you can. Make an announcement in the crew area, too. We'll have to track down any we don't reach before the meeting. Thanks."

N igel greeted the entertainment and cruise staff and directed them to sit in the front rows of the theatre.

Tristan trudged down the aisle and leaned against the stage. He nodded at Nigel seated in the front row. He raised his hand and waited for the crowd to hush.

"I'm sure you are all wondering why I called this emergency staff meeting. Unfortunately, I have some dreadful news to share." Tristan paused and looked down at his feet, trying to keep his composure. "One of our team passed away last night."

A rumble of worry passed through the crowd. They looked around, trying to figure out who was missing.

Tristan raised his hand again, and the crowd settled. "I'm so sorry to break this news to you. Candi seems to have had an allergic reaction to something and passed away late last night."

Nigel leaned back and covered his eyes with his hands.

Mary lurched from her seat and then sank back down. All the color drained from her face. "No! She can't be dead!"

"I'm so sorry to have had to tell you this news." Tristan looked around the theatre. "Does anyone have any questions?"

The staff murmured amongst themselves.

"If you need to talk, feel free to reach out to Nigel or myself and we will get you the support you need." Tristan sat down next to Hayley.

The staff burst into chatter as they discussed the news.

Fernando knelt down in front of Tristan. "I hate to have to ask, but with Candi gone, what do you want me to do about the dance captain's position? We actually rehearsed without Candi this morning, not knowing what was going on when we couldn't reach her, but we have the rest of the cruise to deal with."

Tristan nodded. "For now, can Mary take over? I can see that she is upset, so if she isn't up to it, we'll have to figure something out."

"I'll talk to her." Fernando stood up and walked over to Mary. Fernando kneeled in front of Mary. She sat up and leaned in to hear Fernando.

Her face lit up, and she nodded to him.

Fernando stood up and walked back over to Tristan, Hayley, and Olivia. "She said she's up to taking over lead. Is there anything else you need from me? I need to get everything preset for tonight."

Tristan shook his head. "No, if you need anything from me, let me know."

"Ok, boss." Fernando walked backstage.

"This feels like awful timing, but I have to get something to eat before call time for the show tonight. Would either or both of you want to go with me?" Hayley asked.

Tristan looked at his watch. "I have about forty-five minutes until I have to host pool games. Do you want to grab something at the pool grill?"

Hayley smiled. "Great! Olivia?"

"Oh, you two go. I'll get something later."

"No, come with us."

"Are you sure?"

"Yes!"

Olivia looked at Tristan. He nodded towards the door. "Come on. The more the merrier."

Tristan slipped through a crew door in the theatre's lobby to avoid being repeatedly stopped by guests on their way up to the Lido. Their footsteps echoed as they walked down the crew hallway to the crew elevator. The elevator slowly rose to the pool deck. Olivia reached up and shaded her eyes as they walked out into the bright sunshine.

Passengers filled the pool deck, some sunning themselves and others swimming. The scents of chlorine and suntan lotion filled the air. Children shrieked as they played a game in the pool.

The joyousness of the passengers was in stark contrast to the sadness of the entertainment staff they had just left.

Tristan nodded at the passengers that recognized him as they passed.

They pulled out stools at the grill's bar and sat down with their backs to the pool deck for privacy. Hayley pushed her stool back a little. "What a day."

"Do you think the cast will pull off the show tonight? Between being down a cast member and then the shock of...." Tristan paused and looked around to make sure no passengers were listening. "The shock of Candi's death."

"It's a very professional cast. I think they'll get through the show." Hayley took a sip of her drink. "Frankly, Candi was the biggest drama queen in the group."

Hayley put her drink down. "I shouldn't have said that. I'm sorry."

Tristan waved his hand in dismissal. "No apologies needed. No one wants to speak ill of the dead, but I know Candi wasn't the easiest to work with. You've been awfully quiet, Olivia. Are you alright?"

"It feels inappropriate for me to say anything given my history with Candi."

Tristan cocked his head. "Oh, I had forgotten about her and Peter. That puts you in an awkward place."

Olivia shrugged. "I didn't really have a beef with Candi particularly. Peter is the one who cheated on me. She could have flirted all she wanted and if he'd been a decent guy, he would have ignored the flirting, like you did."

"She might not have been the one that cheated on you, but she cheated on Lorenzo." Hayley put her hand to her mouth. "Do you think anyone has told him yet?"

"Lorenzo?" Tristan cocked his head.

"Candi and Lorenzo were dating. You know him. He's the head waiter. When she signed off the ship, he didn't know. He thought she was going to come back after her vacation. Sophie told me it devastated him when he learned about her and Peter."

"I guess I'm out of the gossip loop." Tristan shrugged.

"Part of being the boss."

"Oh gosh. So when he was at our table making the cherries jubilee...." Tristan smacked his forehead with his palm. "So that is why she knocked into him. I thought it was an accident. All of that went right over my head."

The waiter set their burgers down in front of them.

Tristan looked at his watch. "Good. I still have a few minutes before pool games."

Olivia bit into her black bean burger. Guacamole oozed out of the bun and plopped onto her plate. She picked up a French fry and sopped up the guacamole.

"Ah, Tristan. Oh, Hayley and Olivia, too. How are all you lovely people today? May I join you?"

"Of course, Dr. Kohli. Please, sit down with us." Olivia patted the empty stool next to her.

Dr. Kohli looked at the menu and placed his order. "We had a passenger overheat in the hot tub. He stayed in longer than the recommended time. No sunscreen, so he is very red. I had to do a medical check. My nurse took him down to the clinic to cool down and put some salve on his burn. I figured I might as well get some lunch while I was up here."

"Doesn't seem to matter how many times we remind our guests to put on sunscreen, we get some that forget." Tristan shook his head.

Hayley added. "Or they want to get a tan for when they get back home."

Tristan pushed his plate away and took a sip of his drink. "Sorry you had to deal with that."

"Not a big deal. He's going to be fine after we cool him down. There are worse things."

The group quieted.

"Have you learned anything about Candi's death since we last spoke?" Tristan asked.

"Such a tragedy. So young." Dr. Kohli shook his head and sighed. "I do not have the equipment to do a full autopsy, of course. That will happen when we get back to port. She had been vomiting. She showed signs of respiratory distress."

"Didn't her roommate notice she was sick?"

"Rachel is her roommate. I put her in an accessible cabin to make things easier on her until she is off of her crutches." He bit his lip. "I wish I hadn't done that. If her roommate had been with her, Candi would probably still be with us."

"You couldn't have known, Dr. Kohli." Olivia patted his hand. "You have nothing to feel bad about."

Tristan leaned in. "Vomiting and respiratory distress? Is that what killed her?"

"From the exam I conducted, it appears to me that she had an allergic reaction to something."

"Peanuts?" Olivia asked.

"I do not have any record of a peanut allergy. I checked her on-boarding paperwork. Her medical form indicated a nightshade allergy."

"Nightshade? What is that?"

"Tomatoes, potatoes, aubergine. These are in the nightshade family. Allergies to them are unusual and not generally deadly. Usually, people who are sensitive to nightshades have inflammation or develop a rash. It is common for people with autoimmune diseases to react to nightshades, but it is very rare for those reactions to be fatal. So I am not convinced that is the cause of death."

"Oh!" Olivia touched her forehead. "Candi had a couple of the little quiches at the midnight buffet last night. She asked the waiter if it had tomato and took an asparagus one instead. Is it possible she accidentally got tomato in the quiche she picked?"

Dr. Kohli shook his head. "I can't rule that out for certain, but such a small amount shouldn't have led to death. Thank you for letting me know that, Olivia. I will add it to the paperwork so they can look into it further when they do the autopsy."

Tristan put his napkin on his plate. "On that note, I have to go lead pool games."

"Sorry. I shouldn't have talked about it during our meal."

"Don't be sorry, Dr. Kohli. I am the one who asked you. Obviously, her death is on all of our minds. I'll do my best to put aside my thoughts on Candi and make sure the passengers have fun." Tristan nodded goodbye to Olivia and Hayley. "Ladies."

Tristan walked over to where Nigel was hooking up a microphone. The sun reflected off of his white pants and shoes. He pulled on his blue polo shirt, trying to get some cool air.

Nigel slid the switch on and tapped the head of the microphone with his finger. "Test, test, test." He walked over to the soundboard and adjusted the levels.

"Ladies and gentlemen, Nigel, here, your assistant cruise director." He paused and waited for the crowd to quiet. "Have we got a treat planned for you today! Are you ready for some pool games?"

The crowd clapped.

"Come on, I can't hear you!" He cupped his ear with his hand. "Did I mention we have prizes?"

The crowd cheered.

"That's more like it. Let's welcome to Pool Deck, the best cruise director on the high seas, your host, Mr. Tristan Waterson!"

The sadness that had been on Tristan's face was replaced with a smile. "Who wants to have some fun?"

H ayley heaved a sigh. "I'm so relieved we got through that performance. What a disaster."

"It wasn't a disaster." Olivia gestured towards the front of house. "The audience loved it. You know how the revue show is supposed to go, so the mistakes were obvious to you, but for them, it was their first time seeing it. They didn't know it was supposed to be different."

Hayley put her hands on the dressing room counter and laid her head down. "Crud muffins."

"Crud Muffins!" Chico bobbed his head up and down.

Hayley popped up. "Sorry!"

"It's okay. At least you didn't swear. You can see why we have to be careful not to swear around him. He loves exciting words. It can take months to teach him a new phrase, but he'll pick up a naughty word the first time you say it."

"I try to be careful."

"I know you do, and I appreciate it. The last thing we need is him coming out with a doozy on stage."

"Yeah, that would be even worse than what happened tonight."

"Honestly, Hayley. It really wasn't that bad."

"I was late to my cue. My zipper wouldn't go all the way up. Our blocking was a mess. I almost bumped into Mary three times."

"Almost, but you didn't actually bump into her. I think it all felt worse than it looked."

"I hope so."

"The cast did pretty well, considering the circumstances. It's been a really stressful day for everyone. Hard to concentrate."

"My brain is mush. I know we were supposed to run through the sub trunk tonight after the show, but I don't know if I have it in me." Hayley leaned over and unbuckled her shoes.

"Don't worry about it. We have a couple of days left to get it ready for the show."

"I don't want to let you down. I also don't want to hurt you if I accidentally go left when I'm supposed to go right."

Olivia laughed. "We don't need a mid-air collision on stage. I'll go over my solo stuff tonight."

"Thanks for understanding." Hayley stood up and unzipped her beaded dress. It hit the floor with a thunk. She stepped out of it, picked it up, and hung it on a hanger. "I really hope Rachel is cleared to dance by the next show."

"I hope so, too. Dr, Kohli must think she'll be cleared to perform soon, or he would have sent her home."

"True." Hayley pulled on her yoga pants and sweatshirt and sat down in front of the makeup mirror. She pulled out a makeup wipe and took her eye makeup off. "First Kate and Rachel getting hurt, and then this with Candi. It's like the production show is cursed."

"Be careful. I don't want you to get hurt. With everyone all wound up and stressed, it would be easy for there to be another accident."

Hayley slid on her sneakers. "I was afraid someone was going to get hurt on stage tonight with everything so wonky."

"I'm glad no one got hurt."

"Me too. Are you sure you are alright with me heading to bed?"

"Of course. Chico and I have some work to do. I came up with an idea of teaching Chico to do a card trick, so I thought we'd work on that tonight."

"Oh! That will be so cute!"

"He already does some of the things I need him to do. I just need to teach him the cues to string it all together."

"I can't wait to see it." Hayley pet Chico and gave Olivia a hug goodbye. "See you in the morning."

Olivia pulled out a small table and raised it up as high as it would go. She put a piece of black velvet over it and laid down three playing cards. "Okay, Mister. Here is what we are going to do. I'm going to show you a card. Then I am going to mix it up with the other cards."

Chico cocked his head.

"Your job is to find the card I showed you. Got it?" Olivia showed Chico the Ace of Spades. "Keep your eye on it."

Olivia dropped the card to the table face up and moved the playing cards around. "Okay. Which one is the Ace of Spades?"

Chico slowly waddled over to the cards and looked at them. He looked up at Olivia, trying to figure out what she wanted.

He picked up the Ace of Spades.

"Good!" She handed him a sunflower seed. "Now we'll flip it over so you can't see which one is the Ace."

She repeated the trick, but with the cards facedown.

Chico looked from card to card. He bent down and flipped one over with his beak.

It was a four of clubs.

"Crud Muffin." Chico picked the playing card up, walked over to the edge of the table, and dropped it on the floor. "Uh oh!"

"No! Don't drop it!" Olivia bent down and picked up the card. "Let's try again."

Olivia showed Chico the Ace of Spades. She carefully laid it facedown in the middle of the other two cards and slowly rearranged them.

Chico watched intently. He walked to the cards and flipped one over.

It was the ace of spades.

"Presto!" Chico shouted.

"Good job!" Olivia pulled a sunflower seed out of her pocket and handed it to him.

"Mmmm!" Chico moved the seed around with his tongue. He snapped it in half and swallowed it. He walked back over to the cards and flipped the Ace of Spades over.

He looked at her expectantly. "Treat?"

"No, no treat for that. I have to shuffle them first."

Chico fluffed his feathers and shook them out. He stood on one foot and ran his wing feathers through his beak.

"Chico, this is not the time to groom. Pay attention." Olivia held up the Ace, placed it facedown on the table and rearranged the cards.

Chico studied the back of the three playing cards and picked up one, and tossed it onto the stage floor.

"No, Chico!"

Olivia bent over and picked up the Ace of Spades. She put it on the table with the other two cards. She turned them over with the back of the card showing and slowly rearranged their positions.

Chico gazed at the cards. He waddled over to them and picked up a card. It was the Ace of Spades.

"Good job!"

"That is a heck of a smart bird."

Olivia jumped.

"Ud Muffin!" Chico yelled. Chico turned and dropped the card off the table. "Uh oh!"

"No! Chico, don't drop the card!"

"Alex. You startled us. I didn't see you there."

Alex walked from the wings out on stage. "Sorry, I didn't mean to scare you. I was just doing my final rounds of the night and saw you guys rehearsing. He's really something. Did he just say stud muffin?"

"I'm sure he didn't say that." Olivia glared at Chico. "He just learned the phrase 'crud muffin' from Haley."

"I'm pretty sure I heard him say stud muffin." Alex grinned.

"Don't flatter yourself."

Chico shook his wings and leaned towards Alex. "Ha, ha, ha. I'm a good, good boy!"

"Yes, you are." Alex reached down and put his hand in front of Chico.

Chico cocked his head and looked at Alex. He lifted one foot and slowly put it on Alex's hand. Chico pulled his foot back and looked at Alex. "Treat?"

"Sorry, buddy. I don't have any treats on me. I'll try to remember to bring you something the next time I see you."

"He doesn't need treats."

"No one needs treats, but everyone likes them."

"Ready to go to breakfast?"

"Yes, I'm starving. Dining room?"

"Ooh, good idea. They have French toast this morning. I'll swing by and we can walk over together."

"Perfect. I'll see you in five." Olivia hung up the phone. "No buffet for me this morning, so I don't know what I'll be able to bring back for you, Chico. Let's get your food dish filled up."

Olivia pulled out the bag of parrot pellets and filled his dish. She took his water dish into the bathroom and washed it out. She filled it with bottled water. "Can you refrain from taking a bath in our water dish today?"

Chico ignored her.

Hayley knocked on the door. "Ready?"

They walked to the dining room and sat at a table in the back.

"I'm so glad you were okay with me skipping rehearsal last night. I feel so much better after a good night's rest. How did your rehearsal with Chico go?"

"Okay, I guess. He got the concept of the trick I taught him, but he thought it was a good idea to throw the card on the floor after he picked it up. I don't know what to do to get him to stop."

"Why is that silly bird doing that?"

"You know how he is. He gets notions. I tried to explain that he needed to hold the card up, but he didn't seem to care what I wanted. I got him to do it right a couple of times, but I don't know if I can get him to do it consistently enough to put it in the show right now. He was picking the right card at least. Alex was impressed with how smart he was."

"Oh, he impressed Alex?"

"Don't give me that. He was doing his final rounds and came through the theatre."

"Funny, whenever I've rehearsed late with the cast, he has never once come through the theatre doing final rounds."

"He said he likes animals. He seems like he really likes Chico."

"Smart man. I approve."

"Chico likes him, too. He almost stepped up on his hand."

"Impressive. It took weeks for Chico to trust me enough to come to me."

"Part of having a rescue parrot. Takes a while to earn their trust."

Hayley picked up the vase from the center of their table and sniffed the flowers. "They always look prettier than they smell."

"Probably don't want to overwhelm the smell of the food." Olivia picked up her menu. "Not sure why I'm looking at the menu. I know I'm getting the French toast and fruit."

"The food is good, but it gets pretty predictable when you know what is going to be on the menu each day."

"Ladies, how are you this morning? Would you like coffee?"

"Thank you, Lorenzo." Hayley lifted her cup.

"Olivia?"

"Could I have hot tea?"

"Of course." Lorenzo put the coffeepot on the warmer and brought over a small silver teapot filled with hot water. He placed it in front of Olivia and then brought over a wood box filled with individually packaged tea bags. He held the box open.

Olivia looked over at the assortment and picked one out. "Thank you."

Lorenzo closed the box and put it back. "What can I get you lovely ladies for breakfast?"

Hayley put down her menu. "We both would like the French toast and fruit. Do you know what the fresh fruit option is today?"

"I believe it is orange slices or grapes." Lorenzo wrote their order on his notepad.

Hayley looked at Olivia. "Orange slices?"

Olivia nodded. "Lorenzo, can we have the orange slices with our French toast?"

"Of course." Lorenzo wrote it down. "I'll put your order in."

Hayley and Olivia watched him walk towards the kitchen.

Olivia bit her lip. "Ugh, I didn't think about the orange thing the other night with Candi. I hope he doesn't think we were making fun of him or anything."

Hayley covered her mouth with her hand. "I never even thought of that."

Lorenzo brought out a tray with two plates with silver covers. He grabbed a wooden stand and flipped it open with one hand. Lorenzo put the tray down on the stand and lifted off the silver domes. He put their plates down in front of them. "Two orders of French toast with orange slices. Anything else?"

Olivia touched Lorenzo's hand. "We're sorry about Candi."

Lorenzo nodded. He clasped his hands behind his back and looked straight ahead. "Do you need anything else?"

"No, this looks lovely. Thank you."

Lorenzo pivoted, picked up his tray, closed the stand, and walked towards the kitchen.

"Open mouth, insert foot." Olivia poured syrup over her French toast.

Hayley took a bite. Her shoulders dropped, and she closed her eyes. "Mmmm, this is so good. I'm going to need to go to the gym later so I can eat all of this."

"Sounds like a plan." Olivia poured more hot water from her teapot into her cup.

She took a sip and put her cup down. "Do you think Lorenzo knew Candi was allergic to tomatoes?"

"Tristan told me to check with you and Fernando about scheduling a couple of rehearsals for the production cast." Hayley plopped down in the chair across from Nigel's desk.

"Let me see what we have going on in the theatre today." Nigel pulled out the daily schedule. "It looks like it is empty from noon until 1:30 when I have Bingo in there. Would that work for you?"

"It works for me. We'll need to check with Fernando."

Olivia sat down next to Hayley. "I was just backstage, and he was hanging lights for the show tonight."

"I'll just walk down and talk to him." Nigel stood up.

"We're headed that way. Do you want me to send him up to see you?"

"No, I'll get the Bingo stuff set up now, so I won't be in your way during the rehearsal. I can talk to him when I get there."

Nigel, Olivia, and Hayley walked down to the theatre. Fernando was up on a ladder. One of his stage crew was standing at the light board, turning on the lights so he could focus them.

Nigel looked up at Fernando. "Hey man, we need to get the cast in for a run-through."

Fernando climbed down the ladder and looked at his watch. "When are you thinking? I have to finish setting up the lights for the juggler. He complained they were getting in his eyes when he was juggling last cruise."

"We've got a break now until I'm in here for bingo."

"That's pretty short notice for me to round up the cast."

"I'm sorry, Fernando. I know it is." Hayley ran her fingers through her hair. "But last night was a disaster for me. I'd feel better if we get a quick run-through of the numbers with me and the girls. I can track them down. We don't need the entire cast."

"Oh, okay. That should work. I saw Sara backstage a little while ago. She was sewing one of her costumes that ripped last night."

Hayley, Olivia, and Nigel walked backstage.

"Sara, glad we found you." Hayley pulled up a chair. "Last night was rough. I'd really like to do a run-through of our parts. Would you be ok with going over our numbers if I can find Mary?"

"Sure." Sara put her costume on her lap. "Mary is right there if you want to ask her."

Hayley turned towards the costume closet. Mary was holding her costume from the opening number.

"I'm sorry I didn't see you there."

Mary shrugged.

"Would you be ok with doing a run-through of our numbers for tomorrow night? I don't want a replay of last night."

"I guess." Mary hung her costume up. "Last night seemed okay to me."

"Not to me. I felt like I was going to bump into you guys multiple times."

"What did you think, Nigel? Did you watch the show?" Mary tucked her hair behind her ear.

"I only saw the end. I had to be in the lounge for trivia. But, if Hayley thinks you all need a run-through, then I think you should do one."

"If that is what you think, I'm fine with doing it." Mary sat down at her spot and picked up her dance shoes. "Are you going to stay?"

"Yeah. I have to get bingo set up." Nigel opened the closet and pulled out the bingo equipment.

"I know it has been a hard week with Kate and Rachel getting hurt and then Candi...." Hayley paused. "And us losing Candi. I think we were all a little off last night from the strain. If we do a rehearsal today and feel like we need another, we'll have time to do it tomorrow."

"No problem." Sara put down her sewing project.

They made their way onstage.

"Olivia, can you sit in the front row and let me know if we get off with our blocking?"

Olivia ran down the steps and sat in the center of the front row.

"Fernando, we're ready to go. Can you put on the click track?"

Fernando headed up to the sound booth and signaled that he was ready to go. Hayley nodded. The music to the opening number burst through the speakers.

Hayley looked over her shoulder at the spacing and nodded her head. She turned and faced the front of house. In unison, Hayley and the dancers shifted their weight from foot to foot. The music changed, and they moved together upstage. Hayley held her spot as she sang along to the click track, while Sara and Mary crossed behind her.

Nigel pulled the cart with the Bingo blower through the stage wings and towards the apron of the stage. He walked back to the closet and pulled out the Bingo flashboard.

Mary glanced at the movement of the flashboard and paused.

Sara spun around and knocked into Mary.

"Sorry! Are you alright?" Sara rubbed her shoulder.

Mary held up her hands. "No, I'm sorry. It was my fault. I got distracted."

"Fernando, take us back to where I come in singing." Hayley turned towards Sara and Mary and made sure they were in their positions.

Fernando started the track, and they launched back into their number.

Nigel plugged in his equipment and sat down next to Olivia to watch the rehearsal.

They finished the number and ran offstage.

Hayley walked to center stage. She raised her hand to shield her eyes from the bright lights. "Fern, can we run the first song of the second act?"

"Coming up!"

Hayley, Sara, and Mary danced in time to the music. They moved across the stage together. Hayley reached her mark and stopped. Mary pulled up short narrowly avoiding running into Hayley.

"Sorry! I'm used to being behind you."

"Mary, I feel you aren't really paying attention. I don't want anyone else to get hurt. I think we've had enough of that this week. If you are going to be filling in as lead dancer, you have to lead."

Mary's face flushed bright red. "Sorry, this was all just last minute. I guess my mind wasn't in show mode."

Haley put her hand on her shoulder. "I understand. I just want tomorrow night to go smoothly. If we can't do a clean run-through of our numbers today, we'll have to do another rehearsal tomorrow."

"Of course." Mary looked into the audience and drew in a breath. "I'm ready."

They finished the dance.

Hayley turned towards Mary and Sara. "Thanks. That felt better. Do you think we need another rehearsal, or are you good?"

"That went well." Mary looked at Sara.

"All good."

Nigel stood up. "I need to get the curtain closed and get the Bingo stuff set up. Are you guys good?"

Hayley nodded.

"Do you need help setting up?" Mary looked at Nigel hopefully.

"I'm good, but thanks." Nigel pulled the extension cord over to the outlet and plugged in the equipment. He pushed the button and closed the heavy velvet curtains.

Hayley asked, "Anyone hungry? I'm ready for lunch."

Olivia nodded. "Sounds good to me. Sara? Mary?"

Sara held up the costume she had been repairing. "Thanks, but I want to get this finished."

Mary shook her head no.

"Looks like it is just you and me, Livy. Where do you want to go? Lido, dining room, the grill?"

"Let's do the Lido buffet. I'm getting low on fruits and veggies for Chico. I can grab some there."

"Of course. Chico needs his snacks." Hayley smiled.

They headed up to the buffet.

"Ugh, the line is so long. I figured the lunch rush would be over by now. Do you want to go somewhere else? I can try to get Chico's snacks later."

"No, I don't have anything planned for the afternoon, so I'm not in a rush. I don't mind waiting."

A passenger in front of them flagged down the buffet steward. "Excuse me, my son is allergic to nuts. Can you tell me if there is anything safe for him to eat at the buffet?"

"Ma'am, let me get my shift manager. He will advise you."

He walked into the kitchen and came back to the buffet line a minute later. Lorenzo pushed open the kitchen door a few seconds after.

"Madam, Arif said you had a question?"

The passenger explained her son's allergy to Lorenzo.

"Of course, we can accommodate you. Your child's safety is of utmost importance to us. If you can let me know specifically what your son would like to eat, I will personally make his food in the back, in our dedicated prep area, and bring it out to you."

The passenger placed her son's order and got her own food.

Hayley and Olivia finally got to the buffet and picked up their trays. The buffet steward filled their plates with their choices. Olivia walked to the display of a watermelon with a fish carved on it and picked up some fruit to take back to Chico. They found a table in the corner, away from the crowd.

"Did you get him a mango?"

"Of course. I got a kiwi, too. That will be fun for him to take apart." Olivia wrinkled her nose. "I'll have an enormous mess to clean up when he's done, but he'll have fun."

Olivia put her fork down. "Did you notice Lorenzo was very knowledgeable about how to accommodate that food allergy?"

Hayley shrugged. "I guess. As head waiter, they must train him in it."

"Right, but I am just wondering about Candi not being able to have nightshades. He must have known about it as her boyfriend."

"He probably did, but he didn't serve any to her. He made the cherries jubilee. The other waiter brought over the quiches that had the tomatoes." Hayley took a sip of her iced tea. "It doesn't really matter, anyway. Dr. Kohli didn't think that was why she died."

"I guess."

"Don't do it, Chico!"

Chico tilted his head and looked at Olivia. He walked to the front of the table and dropped the playing card on the floor. "Uh oh! Oh, no!"

"It is an 'Uh, oh!' No! Stop dropping the card!" Olivia raked her fingers through her blond hair and sighed. She sat down on the stage floor and held her head in her hands.

Chico stood on the edge of the table and flapped his wings, begging Olivia to pick him up. "I'm a good boy. I'm a good, good boy!"

Olivia's shoulders dropped. She looked up at him. Tears stained her cheeks. "Chico, please don't drop the card. We're losing half of our show to Peter. I need you to help me if I'm going to have enough material to fill the show."

Olivia shook her head and wiped the tears off of her cheeks. "Why am I talking to you like you are going to understand me?"

Chico launched himself off the table's edge and flew straight down towards Olivia. He landed with a thunk. "Poor bird."

Olivia put her hand in front of him. "Up!" He stepped onto her hand. She brought him to her chest and rubbed his cheek. He settled against her and closed his eyes.

Olivia scooped up some scrambled eggs and plopped them on her plate. She reached for the handle on the silver warmer and lifted the lid on the sausages. She closed the lid and lifted the next. Olivia used the tongs to grab two pieces of bacon and put them on her plate. She picked up a small dish and filled it with cut-up melon. The breakfast buffet in the Officer's Mess didn't have as many choices as the Lido buffet, but it was a lot quicker. Olivia carried her plate to the table and sat across from Hayley.

She looked up at the clock on the wall. The rumble of the thrusters told her they were pulling up to the dock. They had half an hour to eat breakfast while the ship went through customs and then they could disembark.

Tristan stood up. "I've got to run. Sounds like we've docked." He picked up his plate.

Dr. Kohli walked into the Mess and looked around. He caught sight of Tristan and walked towards them. "Tristan, I was looking for you."

"We've docked. I need to run."

"This will only take a moment."

Tristan looked at his watch. "Of course, have a seat." Tristan sat back down.

Dr. Kohli stood next to Olivia. "I have news on Candi."

"Oh." Tristan looked from Hayley to Olivia and back at Dr. Kohli. "It's alright. You can talk. Hold on."

Dr. Kohli sat next to Olivia.

Tristan took his radio off his belt and paged Nigel. "Nigel, I am going to be five minutes late. Can you hold the fort until I get there?"

Nigels' voice came over the radio. "No problem."

"So, what news do you have for me?"

"I'm afraid it isn't good." Dr. Kohli shook his head. "I spoke with the physician who performed the autopsy.

He believes Candi died due to ingesting nightshades."

"I thought you said that a little tomato in a quiche wouldn't be enough to kill her?" Olivia asked.

"That is right. I said that. It is true. It appears that Candi ingested a significant amount of a toxic nightshade. Not just a piece of tomato. She suffered from anaphylaxis." Dr. Kohli shook his head. "He doesn't know yet what specific nightshade it was. It will take time for him to do the testing to figure that out, as this is uncommon."

Hayley pushed her half-eaten tomato omelet away.

"Hayley, you do not need to fear eating a tomato. Even Candi, who had an allergy to them, would not die from eating a tomato. From her files, it looks like she got hives from eating them. Serious, but not deadly. The pathologist will conduct more tests, but it looks like she ingested enough that her throat became swollen and she couldn't breathe." Dr. Kohli shook his head and sighed. "If I hadn't moved Rachel to an accessible cabin, she would have been with Candi and could have gotten her help."

Olivia touched Dr. Kohli's arm. "You couldn't have known."

Tristan cleared his throat. "Dr. Kohli, do you think this was an accident?"

"I can not say for sure, but it seems highly unlikely that someone who knows they have an allergy would accidentally eat enough for this to happen."

A hush fell over the four of them.

Tristan's chair legs scraped against the floor as he stood up. "I have to run and get down to the gangway. Dr. Kohli, can you reach out to Alex? He needs to be updated."

"Of course. I don't have his number on me but I'll call him once I get back to the clinic."

"Oh!" Olivia reached in her pocket and pulled out her wallet. "Alex gave me his card."

Hayley flashed Olivia a smile and raised her eyebrows.

Olivia rolled her eyes. "He gave it to me in case I got in trouble and needed to reach him quickly."

Dr. Kohli picked up the card and wrote Alex's number in his notebook. He handed the card back to Olivia. "While I am glad that Alex gave you his numbers so he could be there if you got in trouble, I would prefer that you not get into any trouble in the first place."

"I try to stay out of trouble, Dr. Kohli." Olivia tucked Alex's card back into her wallet and put her wallet in her pocket.

"I know you do, child, but somehow trouble seems to find you. You haven't gotten bitten or scratched by any wild animals lately?"

Olivia laughed. "No. Not this cruise anyway."

"Excellent. Let's keep it that way." He patted Olivia's shoulder. "Let me call Alex. Oh, never mind."

Dr. Kohli waved to Alex as he entered the Officer's mess.

Alex acknowledged Dr. Kohli and lifted his mug. He put his mug under the spigot and filled it with coffee. The steam rose from the mug. He sat next to Hayley and smiled at Olivia. "Hey Doc, I've only got a minute. What's up? I've got to get down to the gangway."

Dr. Kohli filled Alex in on the autopsy results. "I don't want to think that someone gave her a lethal dose of nightshades, but I thought you should know that it is a possibility."

The color drained from Alex's face. He dropped his head and took a deep breath. "Not how I wanted to start my day. What do you think the chances are that it could have been an accident?"

"Unfortunately, I think that is a very slim possibility. Nightshade allergies are rarely fatal. She would have had to consume a significant amount or one that is toxic." Dr. Kohli shook his head. "I wish I had different news. It was already a tragedy for one so young to die, but to think that it was intentional is quite upsetting."

Alex chugged down the last of his coffee and stood up. "I have to get to the gangway. Thanks for filling me in. I'll let Tristan know when I see him."

"I have already told him."

Alex bit his lip and exhaled. "I'll need to fill in Captain Vasopoulos."

"Yes, that needs to happen as well. I will forward my report to you to share with the necessary parties."

Dr. Kohli followed Alex out of the Mess.

Olivia wrinkled her nose. "Oh gosh. Candi wasn't my favorite person, but it is awful to think that someone killed her on purpose."

"Who do you think did it?"

"I don't want to sound awful, but she sure left a line of people who weren't big fans of hers. It feels like there is a pretty long list of people who had motives." Olivia thought for a second. "Lorenzo is the most obvious suspect. He probably knew about her allergy since they'd dated. She dumped him and then all of the shenanigans with knocking the flaming orange out of his hands. He was pretty upset with her and he had access to her food."

Hayley shivered. "Yuck, we ate the cherries jubilee he made."

Olivia tilted her head. "Do you think he could have hidden something she was allergic to in the cherries?"

Hayley shrugged. "No one else got sick"

"True."

Olivia and Hayley picked up their plates and put them in the tub of dirty dishes.

"I was looking forward to a relaxing day at the beach, but this sure has cast a shadow over the day." Olivia covered her mouth with her hand. "That was so insensitive. Candi is dead. I shouldn't be whining about my day at the beach getting ruined."

14

"It has to be Lorenzo." Olivia leaned forward. "Talk to him, Alex. I think he killed Candi."

"Olivia, we have been over this before. I do not need you investigating or telling me who I need to interrogate. That is my job, not yours. I expect you to stay out of this." Alex picked up a stack of papers on his desk and straightened them. "Am I making myself clear?"

Olivia sank back in her chair and crossed her arms. "Oh, you are making yourself perfectly clear."

"Good. Is that all?" Alex placed the stack of papers in the corner of his desk.

"So you aren't even going to ask me why I think Lorenzo killed Candi?"

"No, I'm not." Alex leaned back in his chair.

Olivia stood up and put her hands on her hips. "I have useful information that will help you with your investigation. It is ridiculous that you won't listen to me." She smacked his desk.

Alex cocked his head and crossed his arms. "Olivia."

"Don't 'Olivia' me!" She stomped her foot. "I wouldn't have come to talk to you if I didn't think I had information that could help you."

Alex stood up and sat on the edge of his desk. "I don't doubt that you could help me. But finding out what happened to Candi is not your job."

"Afraid someone else would get credit for catching him?"

Alex shook his head and threw up his hands. "No. Of course not."

"Then why won't you listen to me?"

"Olivia, I don't want you to get hurt. If you start sniffing around this case, whoever is responsible will not take kindly to it. I don't want you to be their next target."

Olivia's shoulders sank. "I appreciate that you don't want me to get hurt. But I'm not talking about investigating

Lorenzo. I just want to tell you why I think he is responsible for Candi's death."

"Fine. If I let you tell me what you know, you promise to drop this and not talk to anyone about it?"

Olivia nodded.

"You'll stay away from Lorenzo and not question anyone."

"That's all I wanted to do in the first place. I don't know why you have to be so infuriating!" Olivia threw herself back into the chair. "Can I tell you now?"

"Go for it."

"Alright, did you know that Lorenzo and Candi were dating?"

Alex shook his head.

"He thought Candi was going to come back and be with him after her vacation, but instead she took a contract on another ship."

"That's not uncommon. Shipboard romances don't have the best record for lasting."

"I'm aware of that." Olivia cocked her head.

"Candi taking another contract is not a reason for him to kill her."

"I didn't say it was." Olivia exhaled. "Candi didn't just get a new contract by herself. She got a contract with Peter. She was cheating on Lorenzo with him."

"Wait, Peter. Your Peter?"

Olivia wrinkled her nose. "Ugh. Please don't call that jerk my anything. But yes, that Peter."

"If you think that Lorenzo could have killed Candi because she cheated on him, then why shouldn't I look at you as a suspect? Apparently, Peter cheated on you with Candi. Did you want Candi dead for what she did to you?"

Olivia tilted her head to one side. Her eyes narrowed. "Are you actually accusing me of killing Candi?"

She stood up and started for the door.

Alex reached for her arm. "I'm not accusing you of anything. I am just saying that your logic could be applied to you as easily as you are applying it to Lorenzo."

"I wasn't in a relationship with Candi. Peter is the one who cheated on me."

"So if Peter turns up dead, then I should look at you as a suspect?"

"You're really funny. No, Peter cheating on me is probably the best thing that ever happened to me. I should have sent Candi a thank-you card for showing me who he was, so I didn't keep wasting my life on him."

Alex chuckled. "That's one way to handle it."

Olivia rolled her eyes. "I have more reasons why I think he killed her if you want to listen to me instead of fighting with me."

"Proceed." Alex grinned at Olivia.

"Anyway, Hayley and I were at the midnight buffet with Candi before she died. She kept flirting with Tristan. She was doing it intentionally to irritate Lorenzo."

"Okay. Still not a reason to kill someone."

Olivia raised her eyebrow.

"Fine, go on."

"Dr. Kohli told us that it was in Candi's file that she was allergic to nightshades. That is not a common allergy. Wouldn't her boyfriend have known that she had that allergy?"

"Makes sense that he would. But that doesn't mean he killed her."

"You are the most infuriating man I have ever met."

"Thank you."

"I didn't mean it as a compliment."

"I am aware." Alex grinned at her.

"Stop it."

"Stop what?"

"You know what? Never mind." Olivia stood up. "Apparently, I have nothing to offer. Sorry for wasting your time."

"You never waste my time." Alex took her hand and looked into her blue eyes. "Drop it. I don't want anything to happen to you."

Olivia nodded.

Olivia flipped over on her lounge chair and readjusted her towel.

"For goodness' sake, girl, settle down. You haven't laid still for more than three minutes since we got here. Sunbathing by the pool is supposed to be relaxing, remember?"

"Sorry, I just can't seem to relax." Olivia stood up and picked up her towel. "I should go, so I don't ruin your afternoon."

"Livvy, put your towel down. I don't want you to leave." Hayley adjusted the back of her lounge chair so she was sitting upright. "Tell me what has you so worked up."

"It's Candi. I can't stop thinking about what happened to her. I think Lorenzo killed her. Alex totally blew me off when

I told him." Olivia hugged her knees to her chest.

"Alex blew you off?" Hayley cocked her head.

"Alright, maybe he didn't blow me off, but he kept telling me to drop it."

"Why?"

"He said he didn't want anything to happen to me."

"There you go."

"There you go?"

"I knew it. He wasn't blowing you off. He doesn't want anything bad to happen to you." Hayley grinned. "Alex likes you."

Olivia rolled her eyes. "Are we in middle school?"

Hayley looked around the deck and laughed. "Sometimes it feels like a middle school with all the cruise ship drama."

"Valid point."

Hayley signaled a waiter who was walking by and ordered two Pina Coladas.

"This will help you relax." Hayley handed Olivia a drink. "Cheers!"

Olivia clinked her glass to Hayley's and took a sip. Her shoulders relaxed. "So good. You are a brilliant woman."

"I know." Hayley shrugged. "Now, tell me why you are so worked up about Alex."

"I'm not worked up about Alex. I just think he needs to look into Lorenzo. He isn't taking Candi's death seriously."

"I didn't get that at all from what you said. What I heard was that he doesn't want you to get in the middle of this and be in danger. You can be annoyed with me too because I agree with him. I don't want you getting hurt, either."

"Fine. I'm obviously wrong. I'll drop it." Olivia threw the back of her lounge chair down and flipped over onto her stomach.

"Liv, come on. What does it even matter to you after what Candi did?"

Olivia turned her head and laid it on her arms so she could look at Hayley. "Obviously, I don't like what she did. But I don't want her dead."

"I'm not saying you do. But none of this is your responsibility. Leave the investigation to the professionals. Alex knows what he is doing."

"I guess."

"Finish that Pina Colada. Then I'll order you another one."

"Okay, that sounds like a good plan." Olivia flipped over and sat back up. She took a sip of her drink.

"Do you think that Peter even knows about Candi?" Hayley took a sip of her drink.

"I have no idea. He's not my responsibility. Right?"

"Good job. You are right, he isn't your responsibility. Any progress with Chico and his new trick?"

"I wish." Olivia picked the slice of pineapple off the rim of her drink and took a bite. "That reminds me. I need to get him some pineapple before we go down to my cabin."

"We can't forget Chico's pineapple."

"He is doing the first part of the trick perfectly. He watches me so closely. Chico knows exactly what I want him to do. But then he just drops the card onto the stage floor. I have tried everything and I can't get him to stop."

"When we rehearse the sub trunk tonight, you'll have to show me what he is doing. Maybe I can help you figure out a way to get him to stop."

"That would be great. Our show is coming up quickly and we really need that five minutes to fill out our forty-five minutes. I don't feel all that confident in planning out the length of the show.

It would be awful if we ran short and Tristan wasn't there to end the show."

"That would be a disaster. Can you imagine?"

"It would be a total nightmare. Peter was always the one that kept the show moving at the right pace on stage. If we got ahead of schedule, he had a backup trick he could add. I just don't have the experience, or know enough tricks yet, that I feel confident that I can do that."

"Chico! Stop dropping the cherries on the floor!" Olivia bent down, picked up the cherry, and tossed it in the trash. "What is up with you today? You love cherries."

Chico cocked his head and studied Olivia. He reached into his dish and picked up a cherry. He held it up to his beak with his foot.

"Good! That's how you do it." Olivia smiled.

Chico put his foot down, walked to the edge of his cage, and launched the un-eaten cherry to the floor. "Ha, ha, ha."

"It's not funny, Chico." Olivia slumped in her chair. "Why are you doing this? Is there something wrong with the fruit I brought you?"

Chico swayed back and forth on his perch.

Olivia reached into the bowl of fruit she had on her desk and picked up a cherry. She popped it in her mouth.

Chico froze and looked at her.

Olivia swallowed. "It tasted just fine. I don't know what is wrong with you."

Olivia opened up her desk drawer and pulled out a bag of almonds. "Better?" She put three almonds in Chico's dish.

Chico shook his tail feathers out and wiggled down the perch to his dish. He scooped up an almond in his beak and held it with his foot. He used his tongue to find the seam of the almond and split the shell with his beak. "Mmm. Snack."

"Glad you liked it. But you know almonds last a long time and fruit goes bad quickly?" Olivia shook her head. "You are a silly bird."

"Bird! Silly bird!" Chico flapped his wings while he held onto his perch.

Olivia's hair blew back from the wind Chico created. The stack of playing cards she had put on her desk blew off onto the floor. "Thanks. Just what I needed. A birdy hurricane in my cabin."

Olivia knelt on the floor and picked up the cards. She reached to get the cards that had blown under her bunk. Her hand hit a box. Olivia pulled the box out from under the bed. She sat cross-legged on the floor and put the box on her lap. She took the lid off of the box and reached inside.

Olivia picked up a picture of Peter. His face was so familiar, but he was also a stranger. She had thought she knew who he was, but he'd been living a double life behind her back.

"How did I not see what he was doing, Chico?"

Olivia tossed his picture in her trash can and picked up another of her and Peter, smiling on a beach under a palm tree. "What is wrong with me that I didn't know he was cheating on me? We lived together. We worked together. I thought I knew him. I feel like such a fool."

"Ptooey."

"Is that right?" Olivia leaned back against the bed frame.

Chico leaned forward on his perch and shook his wings, begging Olivia to pick him up. "Hey."

Olivia stood up and picked up Chico.

He leaned his head against her chest. "Awww."

Olivia pet him under his wing. "You're a good boy."

Chico settled in, his eyes closed, and his wings sagged as she pet him.

A knock at Olivia's door made Chico jump. "Gadzooks!"

"It's alright, Chico-man. It's probably just Hayley."

Olivia opened the door.

"Want to grab something to eat before we go rehearse?"

"Sounds good to me. Let me put Chico up."

"Shucks!" Chico bobbed up and down.

"Sorry, Chico. I'll bring you some veggies to make up for it, okay?"

Olivia carried Chico back to his cage and put him inside. He tucked one foot up into his breast feathers and closed his eyes.

"Doesn't look like he'll miss me that much. He's ready for a nap." Olivia pulled his cover over his cage. "I'll come to get you for rehearsal after your nap."

"Night, night."

"Good night, Chico."

Olivia shut her cabin door behind them. "I adore that bird."

"Me, too." Hayley smiled. "I never knew parrots had so much personality and were so affectionate until I met Chico."

"He's a love bug. I love him to bits. Although I'm pretty frustrated with him. He was dropping his fruit on the floor today and making a colossal mess. I don't know what is up with him dropping everything. I hope he gets over it so we can put his new trick in the show."

"I do, too. I hope we can figure out why he keeps throwing the card on the floor."

Hayley approached the Maitre'd. "Do you have room for us? Are we too late for dinner?"

"Of course, we have a table for you, miss. Follow me."

He led them to an empty table in the back near the kitchen. They placed their orders with their waiter.

Hayley took a sip of her wine and sighed. "Just what I needed."

"Me, too. Excellent choice."

"Any thoughts on what we can do to get Chico to stop dropping the cards? Could we give him double treats or something?"

"One thing I was thinking...." Olivia froze. Alex walked out of the kitchen and made a beeline to their table. His brows were knit together and his dark eyes bored into Olivia.

"Ms. Morgan."

"Are we back to formal names?"

"If you are going to ignore me and my advice."

"What?" Olivia squinted and shook her head. "I don't know what you are talking about."

"I told you to leave Lorenzo alone, but here you are."

Olivia rolled her eyes. "Seriously? I'm not here for Lorenzo. Hayley and I are grabbing a late dinner before rehearsal. Am I not allowed to eat?"

Alex's shoulders dropped. He took a step back. "I apologize, Olivia. I made an unfair assumption."

Olivia leaned forward and opened her mouth. Hayley reached over and put her hand on Olivia's knee. "Stop."

Olivia leaned back in her seat and crossed her arms.

Alex glanced at the door to the kitchen and then back to Hayley and Olivia. "I hope you both have a lovely dinner. Sorry I interrupted." Alex nodded at Hayley and walked towards the dining room entrance.

"The ever-loving nerve of that man!"

"Liv, stop. Think for a second before you get yourself in a tizzy."

"Think about what? How he falsely accused me?"

"No, not that. Where did Alex come from before he came over to our table?"

Olivia furrowed her brow. "The kitchen?"

"Exactly, the kitchen."

"So?"

"Why would he be in the kitchen?"

Olivia cocked her head.

"Oh my gosh, how could you miss it? He was obviously in there talking to Lorenzo."

"That's why the first thing that came to his head when he saw you there was that you were here to question Lorenzo. Because he had just talked to him and he was doing exactly that."

"Well, I guess that makes sense."

"You know what that means, right?"

Olivia leaned in and shook her head.

"Girl, that means that he listened to you when you talked to him about Lorenzo and he is following up on it. He didn't ignore you." Hayley threw up her hands. "He took you seriously and is looking into what you told him. He respects you and what you said."

"Hmm." Olivia sank back into her chair. "You could be right."

"Could be? Of course, I'm right!"

Olivia laughed. "Of course you are. I should never doubt you."

"Exactly. I am glad you are finally learning that!"

Olivia rolled her eyes and smiled. "It makes me feel better that he questioned Lorenzo."

Lorenzo stalked out of the kitchen. He approached their waiter, who was folding napkins at his station and poked him in the chest with his finger.

Olivia leaned in, trying to hear what he was saying, but he was speaking under his breath.

Lorenzo whipped around and headed back into the kitchen. He banged the swinging door open and pushed past another waiter coming out with a tray of food.

Hayley and Oliva's waiter rolled his eyes and went back to folding napkins.

16

"Oh! I didn't know you were here!" Rachel's crutch clicked on the floor as she hobbled out of the stage left wing.

"Hey! Good to see you up and around. How is your foot doing?"

"Much better, thanks. Dr. Kohli said I should be off of the crutches in a couple of days."

"That's great news!"

"I'm pretty relieved. He said that it is only a minor sprain, but he wants me on the crutches out of an abundance of caution since I'm a dancer and my livelihood depends on my feet being healthy. What you are you guys doing here this time of night?" Rachel steadied herself on her crutches.

"Hayley and I are rehearsing an illusion to put in the show this cruise."

"Oh, that makes sense. I didn't think about you doing that."

Chico held onto his ring stand and flapped his wings.

Rachel lept away from Chico. "Is he going to get me?"

"No, he's just exercising. He won't fly to you unless you ask him to."

"Ask him to?"

Olivia lifted her hand and held it level. Chico sunk low to his perch and flapped his wings. He lept off and flew to her. Chico landed on her hand and panted.

Olivia kissed his head. "We need to do more flying exercises, I think. You shouldn't be out of breath when you fly."

She gave him a sunflower seed and walked him back to his ring stand. "Up!"

Chico stepped onto the perch and used his tongue to move the sunflower seed around his beak as he ate it.

Hayley cocked her head. "Do you need help, Rach?"

"No, just passing through. Thanks, though." Rachel shuffled towards the door. "Good luck with your rehearsal."

"Thanks!" Olivia pulled the case out from behind the back curtain. "Help me lift the lid off."

Hayley grabbed the handles on the opposite side. They pulled the lid up and off of the sub trunk. They put the lid on the floor and then lifted the trunk out of the bottom tray of the travel case.

"I still think having a trunk inside of a trunk is ridiculous."

"If you had paid a couple thousand for the sub trunk, you wouldn't."

"Holy moly! It is just a box. I didn't know it was so expensive."

"None of this stuff is cheap." Olivia gestured towards the rest of her trunks.

"I guess I never thought of the investment you would have to make.

They pay for all the production show stuff. I just show up."

"Peter and I invested a lot of money in our show. Just about everything we made went into upgrading the show so we could get better contracts."

"Pretty infuriating that he thought he could just dump you and take all the stuff you had both worked for."

"He always told me we were partners, but I guess when push came to shove, he didn't really think that." Olivia shrugged. "I guess I'm lucky that he always left the tedious stuff to me. Otherwise, he would have filled out the paperwork to sign off all the illusions, and I wouldn't have had anything but my clothes and Chico. I still can't believe that he thought he could just waltz back on the ship and I'd go back to him like nothing happened."

"I'm proud of you for standing up for yourself."

"Well, I might not have, if you didn't have my back."

"I don't know about that. I think you are stronger than you realize." Hayley gestured around the stage. "Look at all you have done in such a short period of time. I couldn't put together a full-length professional magic show like you are doing. Even if I had all the stuff."

"I guess I absorbed how to do this more than I thought I had." Olivia pulled out the handcuffs. "Ready?"

Nigel walked down the aisle of the theatre and laughed. "Handcuffs? Looks like I arrived just in time."

"Good one, Nigel. We're doing a run-through of the sub trunk and of Chico's new trick."

Nigel looked around the stage. "Ah, I didn't know you two were rehearsing tonight. You need anything?"

"No, we're fine. Thanks though."

Nigel ran his fingers through his dark hair. "How long do you think you are going to be rehearsing?"

"I'm not sure. I guess it depends on how it goes."

"A few of us are going to the crew bar tonight if you finish up early enough."

Hayley wiggled back and forth. "Fun! Thanks for letting us know."

Olivia glanced at the clock in the wings. "We'll see. We have a lot to do to get ready for the show."

Nigel shrugged. "If you see any of the cast, let them know, okay?"

"Rachel was just here, too bad we didn't know then, or we could have told her. I'm sure she is itchy to have some fun after being cooped up hurt."

"Ah, bummer." Nigel looked past Olivia to the backstage area. "Any chance you know where she went? Maybe I can catch up to her and let her know."

"Sorry. She didn't say where she was headed. She left through the dressing room if that helps."

"Alright, I'll have a look and see if she's around. Thanks."

Hayley took the handcuffs from Olivia. "I didn't expect the theatre to be Grand Central Station this time of night."

"Choo, Choo!" Chico chimed in.

"Before we do the sub trunk, should we practice with Chico?" Hayley walked over to him. "We don't want him to get too tired before his turn."

"He's pretty rested from the nap he took while we were eating dinner, but we can do his part first."

Hayley picked Chico up and brought him over to the table where Olivia had set up his trick. She lowered him. "Down."

Chico hopped off her hand onto the velvet table. Olivia picked up the stack of cards, fanned them out, and pulled out the Ace. She showed the Ace of Spades to Chico and then laid the cards face down in a row on the table. She picked up the cards and changed their positions. "Find your card, Chico."

Chico sidled up to the cards and rocked back and forth. He took a step forward and picked up a card.

Hayley clapped. "He did it! He found the Ace of Spades. I had no idea which card it was, and I was watching really closely."

Chico waddled to the edge of the table and dropped the Ace on the floor. "Uh oh!"

"No! Chico! Do not drop the card."

"I'm a good boy! A good, good boy!"

"Good boys don't throw cards on the floor." Olivia bent over and picked the card up. "Any ideas on what is going on in his little bird brain?"

"He said 'uh oh' so he knows he shouldn't drop the card."

"Yep, but he also said he is a good boy, so he doesn't think it is wrong." Olivia threw up her hands. "I wish I knew what he was thinking."

"Shall we try it again?"

Olivia performed her part of the trick and waited for Chico to pick out a card. Chico bobbed his head up and down and then picked up the card. Before Olivia could see what he had chosen, he ran to the edge of the table. Olivia tried to grab the card out of his beak, but he dodged her and dropped it over the edge of the table. It fluttered to the stage floor.

Olivia threw up her hands. "Ugh!"

Hayley bent down and reached for the card. She wiped her hands on her leggings. "Ew. It has something on it."

Olivia took the card from Hayley. "Chico, do you have food on your beak?"

"Treat!"

"No, no treat. You threw the card on the floor."

Olivia picked Chico up and looked at his beak. She took his beak and wiped it with her fingers. "Nope. Nothing there."

"What is this?" Olivia held the card at an angle so she could see it better in the light. "It's shiny."

Hayley knelt down where she had picked up the card and ran her hand over the floor. "There is something on the floor. Did you grease the castors on the trunk?"

"No."

"Weird. I'll let Fernando know tomorrow so he can get it cleaned up. We don't need anyone else falling."

Olivia walked over to her close-up magic case. "Shoot, I don't have another deck of cards with me. I don't want Chico to get whatever that is in his mouth. I guess we'll have to rehearse his trick later when I can get another deck from my cabin."

"You can't just use another card?"

"No, I want him to remember which card he is looking for, so I always use the same one."

"Makes sense." Hayley dangled the handcuffs. "Back to the sub trunk. Ready to run it through, then?"

They ran the trick through three times.

"You are getting pretty fast!" Olivia smiled. "I'm impressed with how quickly you are picking this one up. Especially after you were so nervous about doing the drop."

"Thanks. I'm feeling much more confident."

"Should we do another run-through?"

Hayley bit her lip. "Would it be awful if I said I'd rather not?"

"Of course not. It's been a busy week. You must be tired."

"Actually, I was thinking about going to the crew bar." Hayley scrunched up her nose. "Does that make me an awful person? If you think we need to do another run-through, I'll stay."

"Why would that make you an awful person?"

Hayley shrugged. "I don't want to let you down."

"You aren't letting me down! I wouldn't even be on the ship still if you hadn't stepped up and helped me with the show."

"Never mind. I shouldn't have even mentioned the crew bar. Let's do another run-through."

"Hayley, I'm fine. Really. You should go to the crew bar."

"Are you sure?"

"I'm sure."

"Why don't you come, too?"

Olivia nodded towards Chico. "Chico needs to go to bed and I have to put away all the stuff we pulled out to rehearse with. I still have to get Peter's stuff packed up, and the paperwork filled out to get it off the ship. I have a list a mile long."

Hayley picked up Chico's travel cage. "We'll take him down to your cabin on our way. A night out with friends will be good for you."

"No, go have fun. I've got too much to do."

"It's already pretty late. We won't be at the crew bar for more than an hour. You can take an hour off to have fun." Hayley reached for Olivia's hand. "Please, it'll be more fun if you come."

Olivia looked around the stage at all the stuff that needed to be put away. "But..."

"I'll help you later. Come on. Just take a little break."

"Fine." Olivia picked Chico up and put him in his travel cage. "What the heck, right?"

"Awesome! Help me push the sub trunk into the wings. We'll come back when the crew bar closes and put it back in its case."

Olivia and Hayley took Chico down to Olivia's cabin and tucked him in for the night, then headed to the crew bar.

"You know what? All the years that I've worked on ships, I've never been to the crew bar."

Hayley stopped dead in her tracks. "What? How is that possible?"

Olivia laughed. "I don't know. Peter and I never really did stuff like that. We were on the passenger manifest, so if we went out, it was to have a cocktail in one of the lounges, but we didn't really drink much. Mostly, we'd just hang out with the other headliners in the Lido buffet after it had closed. It was a nice quiet place to visit."

The metal walls vibrated from the bass music coming from behind the door.

"Wow. Sounds exciting. That was sarcasm if you didn't catch it." Hayley pushed open the door. "Liv, prepare yourself for some real fun."

The low-ceilinged room smelled of stale beer.

It took a few seconds for Olivia's eyes to adjust to the dark after the bright hallway.

A few officers stood at the small bar having a drink, and a group of engineers were playing pool. In the corner, a DJ was set up in front of a mirrored wall. Colored lights flashed in time to the music. Crew members and staff, some in uniform, but most in their civilian clothes, sat around drinking and laughing.

Hayley grabbed Olivia's hand and pulled her towards a table in the corner where members of the cast and cruise staff sat drinking. She motioned for Olivia to sit down in an empty chair. She pulled over a chair from another table for herself.

Hayley leaned in towards Olivia. "I'll grab you a drink at the bar. What do you want?"

Olivia looked around the table. Everyone had cans or bottles of beer. "A beer, I guess."

"Good choice." Hayley winked at her and walked up to the bar. She came back with two bottles of beer with a lime stuffed in the neck.

"Cheers!"

They clinked bottles.

Olivia watched Hayley shove the lime down the neck of her beer. The lime bobbed around as the beer fizzed up. Hayley took a sip and her shoulders dropped. "Ah!"

Olivia pushed her lime in. The juice ran down her fingers. She licked the juice off and took a sip.

Hayley elbowed her and motioned across the table with her beer.

Nigel was saying something to her, but she could hardly hear him over the music. She leaned in and cupped her ear.

"How did your rehearsal go?"

"Oh, sorry. It's loud in here. Good. It went well." Olivia took a sip of her beer. "Glad you caught up with Rachel."

Rachel smiled at Olivia. "Thanks for letting him know which way I had headed. I'm so slow on these crutches he caught me before I got to the elevator."

"I wouldn't give up that easy. If I had missed you at the elevator, I would have kept looking." Nigel grinned at Rachel.

Mary reached across the table and grabbed a handful of chips out of the open bag. Her elbow grazed Rachel's beer. It wobbled back and forth fell onto the table. Rachel scooted back from the table as beer dripped down into her lap.

Nigel picked up the beer bottle and sat it upright.

"Sorry." Mary took the cocktail napkin out from under her beer and handed it to Rachel.

"It's alright. Accidents happen."

Nigel jumped up and ran to the bar. He came back with a new beer and a stack of napkins.

Rachel took the napkins from Nigel and blotted the beer off of her skirt.

Mary shrugged and leaned over her drink.

The DJ transitioned the dance party music into a slow dance.

Nigel leaned in and asked Rachel to dance with him. She motioned towards her foot.

"I'll hold you up." He stood up and took her hands, pulling her up from her seat. "You can lean on me."

He led her to the dance floor and held her tightly as they rocked to the music.

"Another shipboard romance." Sara took a sip of her beer.

"Aw, I didn't know they were a thing." Hayley finished her beer and put it down on the table.

Mary shrugged. "He's probably just being nice to her since she hurt her foot."

Nigel leaned down and kissed the top of Rachel's head.

"I don't know, that looks like love to me." Hayley grinned. "Is there anything sweeter than when a man kisses the top of your head? It is so romantic it makes my heart flutter."

Olivia cocked her head. "I don't think I've ever had a man kiss me on top of my head like that."

"What?" Haley's mouth hung open. "Peter never kissed you like that?"

"Not that I can remember."

"Good lord, everything I hear about that man makes me dislike him even more."

"He wasn't the most romantic guy, I guess."

"You deserve better."

"Don't we all?"

Hayley walked up to the bar to get another round.

Mary slouched against the wall, watching Nigel and Rachel rock back and forth. Rachel leaned all of her weight on Nigel and held her injured foot off the ground as they swayed.

Olivia picked up her beer and chugged the rest of it down.

Hayley walked over and handed a beer to Olivia, Sara, and Mary.

Mary shoved the lime in with her thumb and drank half the beer in one gulp.

"Whoa there. Slow your roll, lady, or you are going to have a headache in the morning."

"What does that matter?" Mary took another sip and slammed the bottle onto the table.

Hayley furrowed her brow and shrugged her shoulders. "Okay."

The song ended, and Nigel and Rachel came back to the table. Rachel's cheeks were flushed pink.

"We're going to head out. I'm going to walk Rachel back to her cabin. I have to get some stuff set up for tomorrow morning. Bingo is at 8 am again. Early morning."

"The life of an Assistant Cruise Director, always getting the early duties that the Cruise Director doesn't want to do." Hayley laughed.

"Isn't that the truth? Maybe you can put in a good word for me with Ol' Tristan."

"Why would my word have any weight?" Hayley shifted in her seat. "Anyway, thanks again for the invite."

Nigel picked up Rachel's crutches leaning against the wall behind her chair and handed them to her. "See you tomorrow."

"We probably need to finish these beers and head out, too." Hayley gestured with her beer towards the bar. "Looks like the bartender is getting ready to close."

"Thanks for the beer." Mary stood up and walked out of the bar.

Sara rolled her eyes and drank down the rest of her beer. "I'm going to ask that cute officer if he wants to dance. I'll see you later, ok?"

Olivia took a sip of her beer. "Mary didn't seem thrilled about Rachel and Nigel."

"I don't think she's ever been a big fan of Rachel's."

"Rachel is so sweet."

"Yeah, but Rachel is also a better dancer."

"Mary is a talented dancer." Olivia took another sip of beer.

"Technically, she can't be beat. But she just doesn't have the same spark that Rachel has. If she would just relax and enjoy performing more, she'd probably have gotten a lot further in this business."

"She's still young. She has time." Olivia shrugged.

"She's not young for a dancer. She's 29. Not much longer to be a professional dancer at that age."

"I guess I thought she was younger."

"Nope, she was talking about her birthday last week backstage. She's 29." Hayley polished off her beer. "Ready to head back to the theatre and put the sub trunk away?"

Olivia put her beer down. "Sure."

"Come on, there's almost half a beer left. Drink it down. Don't waste beer!"

Olivia rolled her eyes, but lifted the beer up to her lips and drank the rest down. The bottle hit the table with a thunk.

"Whew, the fizz got me." She reached up and rubbed the bridge of her nose.

Hayley laughed. "I thought you went to college."

"I did. What does that have to do with anything?"

"How did you get through four years of college without learning how to chug a beer?"

"Three years, actually. I graduated in three years. I was busy, I guess."

"You know what they say. All work and no play....."

"Ready?"

"You sure we shouldn't get another beer?"

"Funny girl, let's go put the sub trunk away so we can get some sleep."

"Fine."

Hayley gathered up their empty bottles and deposited them on the bar. "Thanks, Claudio."

"You know the bartender's name? How often do you come here?"

"Pretty often. I like that I can kick back and have fun and not worry about behaving in a certain way for the passengers. Once they recognize me from the show, it changes things."

"I get that. Thankfully, my show is usually later in the cruise, not opening night like yours. I have a few days where no one recognizes me. After the show, I try to put my hair up or wear a hat when I'm out. That usually worked if I was alone. But if I was out with Peter, he ate up the attention. He would look everyone right in the eye, hoping they would recognize him."

"I'm not surprised to hear that. Performing makes me so happy. I love the little bit of fame I have on the ship. But I also really like to just hang out in the crew bar and not worry about my hair being perfect or wearing a fancy dress to look right for the passengers." Hayley pushed open the heavy door. "I can just be myself."

"Be yourself, huh? What are you ladies doing out so late?"

"Hey." Hayley's face lit up and then dimmed. "We were just leaving."

"And I just got here. Want to have a drink with me?"

"I think Claudio was closing up."

Tristan looked at his watch. "We have 15 minutes. Time for one drink."

Hayley looked at Olivia.

"You guys go ahead. I'm going to go put some stuff away that we left out on stage."

"I should help Olivia." Hayley stepped toward Olivia.

"Don't be silly. I can handle what is left to do." Olivia smiled. "Go have fun. All work and no play, and all that."

"If you're sure?"

"I'm sure." Olivia held the crew door open and gestured for Hayley and Tristan to walk through. "See you tomorrow."

The theatre was dark and still. Olivia loved the feel of having the enormous room all to herself. She breathed in the familiar scent. She touched the edges of the seat backs as she carefully walked down the dark aisle.

She made her way to the steps leading backstage. The backstage area was pitch black. The ghost light had been on when she and Hayley had left the stage, but it wasn't lit now.

Olivia felt her way towards the light switch on the back wall. She winced as her toe caught on the thick metal counterweight at the bottom of the rope used to open and close the stage curtain. She held the rope in her hand to steady herself and slowly felt her way along the line of rope rigging.

The curtain leg brushed her bare arm as the ship hit a wave.

Olivia rubbed the goosebumps on her arms.

A thud stopped her in her tracks. She paused and listened. She must have knocked something when she touched the rigging.

Olivia cautiously took another step forward, reaching for the next rope. The complete darkness disoriented her. She stopped, hoping her eyes would adjust to the darkness.

Something scraped along the stage floor.

She stopped in mid-step, her foot barely touching the floor. She held her breath, trying to not make a sound. Olivia waited a few seconds that seemed like minutes.

The theatre was dead quiet.

She let out her breath, deciding that she had just gotten herself spooked from being in the dark.

She ran her hand along the ropes as she made her way to the light switch on the wall next to the dressing room door.

She felt along the wall, found the switch for the work lights, and flipped it on. She squinted at the row of cold blue lights that dimly lit the back wall of the theatre.

Olivia walked stage right where she and Hayley has shoved the sub trunk.

The lid of the trunk lifted an inch and slammed back down.

Olivia froze.

A muffled 'Help!' came from inside the trunk.

"Who is there?" Olivia's voice quavered.

"Help!" The trunk shook, and the lid lifted a tiny bit again. "Is somebody out there? Help me!"

Olivia recognized the voice.

"Nigel? Is that you?"

"Help!"

Olivia raced to the trunk and threw open the lid. Nigel was on his back with his legs tucked into his chest. His broad shoulders filled the width of the trunk.

She fumbled, trying to get the handcuffs loosened. "They're so tight I can't get them open. Hold on." She grabbed Nigel by the arm and pulled him to a sitting position.

He rubbed the sweat off his forehead with his handcuffed arms.

Olivia ran to her close-up magic trunk and found her extra handcuff key. She dashed back to Nigel and opened the handcuffs. They dropped to the bottom of the trunk. She reached for his hand to help him out.

Nigel pulled away from her and rubbed his wrists. He panted. "Why on earth did you do that to me?"

"Get you out of the trunk?"

"No, of course not. Why did you put me in it?"

"Put you in the trunk? I didn't put you in it."

Nigel stepped away from Olivia and looked around the stage.

"You're the only one here as far as I can see."

"Nigel, you can't really think I put you in the trunk."

Nigel backed away. "What is wrong with you? Is this your idea of a joke?"

Olivia gulped and shook her head. "No, this isn't a joke. I didn't put you in there." She stepped towards Nigel.

"Get away from me. I'm going to call security." Nigel backed towards the Bingo table shoved in the corner of the stage. He picked up his radio.

"You don't need to call security. I mean, call security, but not on me. I didn't lock you in there."

Nigel pushed the button on the side of his radio. "Charlie, Charlie, Charlie. Security needed on stage in the theatre."

Olivia took a step back and knocked into the trunk.

"Just stop right there. Don't move. Security will be here in a second. Stay right there."

"Nigel, this is bananas. I didn't lock you in the trunk. How can you think I could do that?" Olivia wrung her hands.

"Explain yourself to security."

Light flooded the auditorium as Victor, a security officer, pushed open the door and made his way down the aisle. "Sir, what's the issue?"

"This nut job magician pushed me into one of her magic trunks and locked me in there."

Olivia shook her head. "No!"

Victor pulled his radio off his belt. "Ballas, I need backup in the theatre."

He made his way on stage, not taking his eyes off of Olivia. "Miss, can you explain to me what happened?"

"I didn't lock him in my trunk. I don't know how he got in there." Olivia's eyes darted between the men. "I just helped him get out."

Victor looked at Nigel and back at Olivia. "Let's just hold tight until Officer Ballas arrives."

Nigel rubbed his wrists where the handcuffs had dug in.

"Nigel, I didn't do this to you. This is ridiculous." Olivia took a step forward.

Victor put his hand on his belt. "Ma'am, please stand still."

Olivia threw up her hands.

He lurched towards her. "Do not take another step."

Olivia closed her eyes and took a breath. The shallow breath pulled on her tight chest and she almost coughed. Her heart was pounding so hard it hurt.

Her eyes stung from tears, but she didn't dare wipe them away. She didn't know if security had a taser or a gun, and she didn't want to find out.

The sound of running in the lobby got Olivia's attention. She breathed a sigh of relief when Alex appeared through the auditorium doors.

"Alex!" Olivia lurched forward, waving at Alex.

Victor stepped in front of Olivia and blocked her with his arm. "Ma'am, do not move. Wait here for Officer Ballas."

Nigel jumped off the stage and rushed to Alex. He gestured towards the stage, pointing at Olivia. Alex glanced up at her and then leaned in towards Nigel, listening to his story. He reached up and put his hand on Nigel's shoulder.

Olivia's chest contracted again. She had thought everything would be better when Alex got there. Instead, she was afraid he believed Nigel.

Not that she could really blame either of them. How on earth had Nigel ended up in her trunk? Olivia's heartbeat pounded so loudly in her ears that she didn't hear Alex say her name.

Alex touched her shoulder. "Olivia."

Olivia jumped and sucked in air. Her breath shuddered out of her chest as her brow knit together. "Alex." Olivia bit her bottom lip as a tear escaped her eye and ran down her cheek.

"Olivia. Nigel told me what happened."

"No, Nigel told you what he thinks happened. But I swear, I didn't do what he's accusing me of doing."

Alex crossed his arms, one eyebrow lifted, as he cocked his head to one side. "If you didn't, who did?"

O livia opened her mouth to answer.

"Victor, I'll handle it from here. Please escort Nigel to his cabin before you return to your station."

"Yes, sir." Victor nodded his head at Alex. He walked toward Nigel and lead him out of the auditorium.

Alex turned his attention back to Olivia.

"You believe me, don't you?"

"Follow me. We're going to go to my office and I am going to try to figure out what happened and how you ended up in this mess. Again."

She glared at Alex under her furrowed brow. "Why are you always so quick to think the worst of me?"

"Why are you always in the middle of trouble?"

Olivia pursed her lips.

Alex turned on his heel and walked offstage.

"Stop!"

Alex turned.

"I came here to put away the sub trunk. Give me a minute to do that and then I'll go answer all of your... questions."

Alex put his hand up. "No!"

"No?"

"Do not touch the trunk. It is evidence."

"You have got to be kidding me? I don't think Tristan will be thrilled when he comes here in the morning and the trunk is sitting in the middle of the stage."

"I don't think Tristan will be thrilled when he hears that his assistant Cruise Director was assaulted and shoved into your magic trick."

"Of course, he won't be happy about that."

"My staff will secure the trunk. I will not leave it on stage." Alex waved his hand to direct Olivia off the stage.

Olivia glanced back at her trunk and then at Alex. "Fine. It's an expensive piece of equipment and I need it for my show."

"I understand."

Alex led Olivia to his office. He unlocked his door and held it open for Olivia.

Olivia threw herself down in the guest chair in the tiny, bare office. Stacks of paper were organized on the desk in neat piles. Olivia looked around the cramped, windowless space. The walls were bare except for framed diplomas with his name on them.

"No pictures at all?" Olivia asked.

Alex shook his head.

"No pictures of your girlfriend or wife?"

"I don't have a girlfriend or wife."

Olivia bit her lip. "Or your mom?"

"I use this office to question people who have done things they shouldn't have done. I don't really want to involve my mother in that."

Olivia shrugged. "I guess that makes sense."

"Any more questions?"

Olivia rolled her eyes. "No, but I am sure you have some for me."

"That I do." Alex pulled out a pad of pepper and a pen. "Tell me about your evening."

"Fine. Hayley and I had dinner. But you know that since you yelled at me in the dining room."

Alex cocked his head and raised his eyebrows. "And then?"

"And then we came to the theatre to run the sub trunk a few times."

"Run the sub trunk?"

"Sorry. Yes, we are adding the substitution trunk into the show. Basically, Hayley locks me in the trunk, and then she gets on top, lifts a hoop of fabric and when she drops the hoop, I'm standing on top of the trunk and she's locked inside."

"How do you get outside and she gets inside?"

"Good try, but no dice. I will not tell you how the trick works."

"I don't care how the trick works. I'm trying to understand how it works in case it impacts how Nigel was shoved into it and locked up."

"I guess if it comes to that, I'll have to show you how it works in detail, but you asked me what I did tonight and I am trying to tell you."

Alex leaned back in his chair. "Proceed."

"We were trying to run the trick, and we kept having people come backstage. Rachael was there on her crutches and then Nigel came in a few minutes later."

Alex sat up. "Nigel?"

"Yes, he came by and told us he was going to the crew bar with a few of our friends if we wanted to stop by and hang out."

Alex jotted down a note.

"So, did you go to the crew bar?"

"Eventually. We had to practice Chico's new trick a few times and then do the sub trunk."

Alex smiled. "How is Mr. Chico?"

"Actually, he's being a real twit. He's doing the card trick part perfectly, but then he keeps dropping the card on the stage. He dropped it in some gross goop that was on the floor."

"Goop?"

"Yeah, like some oily stuff. I didn't want him to touch it and accidentally ingest whatever it was, so we stopped practicing with him. I hoped Hayley could figure out why he kept dropping the card."

"Did she?"

"No. We were going to run the sub trunk a few more times, but she really wanted to take a break and hang out in the crew bar."

"Did that bother you?"

"No, why would it?"

"Because you have a show to put on and you want to do your best?"

"I do, but I know Hayley. She always does her best. We've run the trick a bunch of times this week. I have confidence in her."

"Alright, so you went to the crew bar. Did you put the trunk away before you went there?"

"No, I guess we should have, but we wanted to have some time at the bar before it closed. Hayley said we'd come back and put it away on our way to bed."

"Okay. What happened at the crew bar?"

"Nigel, Rachel, Mary, and Sara were there. We sat with them. Nigel and Rachel slow danced. We had a couple of beers and then Nigel said he was going to take Rachel back to her cabin and set up the Bingo stuff for tomorrow."

"You knew Nigel was going to be in the theatre?"

"Yes, I guess so. That's where he hosts Bingo."

"So where was Hayley when you came back to the theatre? Why wasn't she with you?"

"We were leaving the crew bar, and we ran into Tristan. He wanted to have a drink."

"Why didn't you stay and have one with him?"

"He didn't really want to have a drink with me. He wanted to have one with Hayley."

"Why not? Do you and Tristan have a poor relationship?"

"Think about it for a second, Alex. You know why."

Alex looked at Olivia blankly.

"Her personality. That copper hair, beautiful figure, and legs that won't quit."

Alex shrugged.

Olivia laughed. "Dude, he has a crush on her."

"Her and not you?"

"He and I don't have a relationship like that. He doesn't think of me that way."

"Okay. If you say so." Alex's dark brown eyes pierced hers.

"Um." Olivia's stomach flipped. "So I left Hayley with Tristan and went to the theatre. All the lights were off. I made my way to the back of the stage to turn on the work lights and I heard a noise."

Alex paused from taking notes. "What kind of noise?"

"A scraping, I guess. When I got the lights on, I could see the lid to the trunk wiggling. That's when I heard Nigel's voice coming from inside."

Alex wrote that down and looked up at Olivia. "Go on."

"I opened up the trunk and helped him out. He had my friction cuffs on, but they were too tight to get off him, so I had to use my key. Then he started yelling at me that I had locked him in the trunk. I swear. I didn't."

"We're back to the question then. If you didn't do it, who did?"

"I don't know. He left with Rachel. She knew he was going to be there. Mary and Sara knew."

"Why would any of them lock him in your magic trick?"

"I have no idea." Olivia held up her hands. "Why would anyone lock him in the trunk? It could have been anyone.

No one was on stage. The lights were out. It's late. Anyone could have been on stage and pushed him into the trunk. It was probably just a practical joke."

"But he wasn't just pushed into the trunk. They handcuffed him before they pushed him in. Someone didn't want him to get out easily."

"I guess that is true." Olivia sighed. "All I know is that I didn't do it."

"Do you have feelings for Nigel?"

"What?" Olivia rubbed her face.

"I'm asking if you have romantic feelings for Nigel."

"Of course not."

"Were you jealous that he slow danced with Rachel?"

"No. Why would I care about that?"

"You followed him to the theatre."

"I didn't follow him. I just went there to put away the trunk so it wouldn't be there in the morning when he did Bingo."

"Were you jealous of Candi and her relationship with Peter?

"Are you kidding me? You're bringing that up?"

Alex shrugged. "Candi had a relationship with your boyfriend and she ends up dead. Nigel slow dances with Rachel and he ends up locked up in your magic trick."

"How dare you? You are disgusting. I can't believe you are accusing me of hurting either of them. Candi did me a favor. She showed me who Peter really is. She kept me from wasting any more time on that...." Olivia's face turned beet red. "She kept me from wasting any more time on Peter and that relationship. Nigel is just a friend. At least, I thought he was. I don't have any romantic feelings for him. I am happy for him and Rachel."

"Rachel was injured in the revue show and you were backstage. Why were you there?"

"Are you freaking accusing me of hurting Rachel now? What is wrong with you?" Olivia ran her fingers through her hair and covered her mouth with her hand. She forced herself to take a deep breath. "I would never intentionally hurt anyone. I did not put Nigel in my magic trick."

Alex leaned back in his chair and crossed his arms. His dark brown eyes locked with her blue
ones.

"It's late." Alex unfolded his arms, stood up, and gestured towards his office door. "Go get some rest. I will interview Nigel in the morning. If I have more questions, I will follow up with you then."

Olivia opened her mouth.

Alex sat back down at his desk and pushed his notepad off to the side. "Yes? Is there something else?"

Olivia hated feeling dismissed like she was a child who had gotten into trouble and been called to the principal's office.

Alex barely looked at her.

His eyes seemed to be focused on the air in between them instead of her face.

Her shoulders dropped. "Fine."

She turned on her heel and fled his office.

The sound of pounding on her cabin door woke Olivia. She jumped out of bed and threw on her robe.

"Uh oh! Oh no!" Chico mumbled in his cage under his dark cover.

"Thanks for stressing me out, Chico."

Olivia walked to her door and peeked through the peephole. She let out a sigh of relief when she saw Fernando standing there. She turned the lock and opened the door.

"Hey, what's up?"

"Sorry to wake you, but Tristan wants to see you asap."

Olivia scrunched up her nose. "Ok, thanks for letting me know. I'll shower and get dressed. Then I'll come up to his office."

"You might want to make it quick. He didn't seem in the best state of mind and I don't think he wants to be kept waiting. That's why he had me come get you when you didn't answer your phone."

Olivia glanced at her phone. "Yeah, I had to turn off the ringer. Chico learned the ring. I kept answering the phone, and it was just him."

Fernando chuckled. "Sounds like something Chico would do."

"Ha, ha, ha!" Chico laughed from his cage.

Olivia shut the door and pulled the cover off of Chico's cage. "You got me in trouble, bird. Tristan couldn't reach me because I had my ringer off."

"Uh oh!"

"That's right. Uh oh. You can be a real pain in the behind, Chico-man."

"I'm a good boy." Chico turned his head and looked at her with one eye. "I'm a good, good boy."

"You have your moments." Olivia pulled out underwear and grabbed a sundress from her closet. She took a quick shower and twisted her hair up into a bun. She filled Chico's food bowl and gave him fresh water. "That ought to hold you. I'll be back soon."

She shut her door behind her and turned, almost bumped into her cabin steward, Joseph.

"Are you going to be gone for a while? Should I do your cabin service now, ma'am?"

"Sure, that works for me. Thank you, Joseph."

"My pleasure."

Joseph used his master key card to open her door.

"Helloooo!" Chico sang.

"Hello, birdie. How are you today?"

"Treat?" Chico asked.

"Maybe just one, my friend."

Olivia smiled at Joseph and Chico.

She remembered she was on her way to Tristan's office, and the smile fled her face. Not the best start to a day.

She trudged up the stairs. He was on the phone. She stood in the doorway, waiting for him to notice her. He waved her in.

"Yes, sir. I appreciate that." Tristan nodded. "Of course."

The dark circles under Tristan's eyes looked almost like bruises. His blonde hair was usually neat as a pin, but this morning it looked like he hadn't brushed it.

He leaned his elbow on the arm of his chair and rested his forehead against his hand.

"Nigel told me about last night."

Olivia sighed.

"Well?"

"There was a misunderstanding."

"Nigel misunderstood that you shoved him in your magic trick?"

"Well, yes. That is what he misunderstood. I didn't do it. After I left you and Hayley, I went to the theatre to put the trunk away. He was in the trunk when I got there. I didn't do it."

"Who else would put him in your magic trunk?"

"Your guess is as good as mine. All I can say is that I didn't do it."

"Nigel is extremely upset."

"I understand why he would be. If someone had done that to me, I'd be upset, too."

"You know, it would be easier for me if you just admitted you did it and apologized to Nigel."

"I'm sorry. I can't do that, because I didn't do it."

Tristan rubbed his eyes. He picked up his phone and dialed. "Fernando, I need all the entertainment and cruise staff in the theatre's auditorium at 1pm today. Can you arrange that?"

Tristan put down the phone and leaned back in his chair. "Are you sure you don't want to tell me what happened here in the privacy of my office, instead of in the theatre in front of your peers?"

Olivia's cheeks flushed. "As I told you and Alex, I didn't do it. Frankly, I'm pretty upset you would think that I would do that to him."

"Let's hope someone fesses up at the meeting. This is the last thing we need in the entertainment department."

"Understood. Anything else?"

"No. I'll see you at the meeting, correct?"

"I'll be there."

Olivia headed down the stairs, taking them two at a time. She felt a rush of hot shame come over her, even though she had done nothing wrong.

She knocked on Hayley's door.

Hayley opened the door and Olivia burst through, flinging herself into Hayley's desk chair.

"What on earth is up with you?" Hayley pulled her blanket up over her sheets, smoothed it, and sat on her bunk.

Olivia caught Hayley up on what had happened since she'd seen her the night before.

"Weird! He was inside the trunk when you got there?"

"Yep."

"Did you see or hear anyone when you got to the theatre?"

"No, it was dark. I was concentrating on getting on stage so I could turn on the work lights. I didn't hear anything until I was on stage. Then I heard him in the trunk."

21

The entertainment staff hushed as Tristan walked on the apron of the stage. Fernando handed him the microphone and then walked down the steps into the auditorium. "Thank you all for coming. I know this was last minute."

Many of the group were sitting in the same seats they sat in when they had learned about Candi dying just a few days before.

Olivia could feel the nervous energy vibrating off the people sitting near her. She glanced around at the rest of the staff sitting in the first few rows of the auditorium.

Fernando scanned the faces of his co-workers. He caught Olivia's eye and froze. He quickly glanced away.

Olivia leaned in and whispered to Hayley. "Everyone thinks I hurt Nigel. I hate this."

"Don't be silly. No one is thinking that."

Olivia looked at Nigel sitting in the front row with Rachel, Sara, and Mary. He was glaring at her. Nigel leaned forward, but Rachel put her hand on his arm, settling him down. He leaned back in his seat.

"Nigel is thinking that."

"We'll just have to figure out who pushed him in."

"How are we going to do that, Hayley?"

"I don't know yet. Maybe Tristan has a plan, and that is why he called this meeting."

"He's hoping someone fesses up."

"Well, maybe someone will. It was probably just a sick joke."

Tristan glared at Hayley.

She stopped talking and settled back into her chair. She looked down at her hands in her lap.

Tristan cleared his throat. "We had an incident late last night. After this meeting is over, we'd like to meet with each of you individually for a minute to discuss where you were and if you saw anything that could help us."

Tristan looked over Olivia's head. "Officer Ballas and I will call for each of you. Please stay in your seat and wait until we talk to you after the meeting is done."

Olivia looked behind her. Alex sat two rows back. He gave her a stony stare before he scanned the crowd.

"On to other news. Much better news." Tristan exhaled. "I know that this has been a very stressful week for all involved."

A rumble of speculation ran through the staff. Tristan raised his hand to silence them.

"I spoke with Dr. Kohli late this morning. He has cleared Rachel to perform."

The audience clapped for Rachel. Nigel put his arm around Rachel's back and patted her shoulder.

Tristan nodded at Rachel. "We are all so relieved that you can come back and perform with the production show cast."

A group of cruise staff whistled and cheered behind her. "Go, girl!"

Mary sat with a blank expression, while everyone around her was cheering. She folded her arms and stared in front of her. Sara patted Rachel's knee and smiled.

"In honor of Rachel returning to the show tonight, plus a big announcement I will be making. I want to invite you all to join me on stage after the final curtain tonight. I spoke with the head chef and he's having his baking staff make a special cake for us to share."

Olivia laughed at the shouts of excitement coming from the entertainment staff. "Goodness. You would think they didn't have access to free cake every single day, sometimes multiple times a day, on the buffet."

"True, but I think it's not really the cake. It is celebrating something happy finally happening on this cruise."

"True."

Tristan tapped the microphone to get their attention. "Settle down, folks. I'm glad you're happy, but it is just cake."

Olivia whispered. "I forgot to ask, how did your date go last night?"

"He's talking." Hayley shushed her. "And it wasn't a date."

A ripple of laughter swept through the small crowd.

"Before I dismiss you, we need to take care of business. Starting with Fernando, I'd like each of you to come to the back, one by one, and answer just a couple of questions on your way out. After we speak with Fernando, he'll come to get you when it is your turn." Tristan covered his heart with his hand. "I appreciate all of you and the work you do. Thank you."

Tristan fished the microphone into the mic stand and walked down the stage steps.

Olivia caught a flash of white behind her as Alex stood up and walked up the aisle to meet Tristan.

"This is going to be miserable. I've already talked to both Alex and Tristan. I wish they'd just let me leave instead of sitting here with Nigel glaring at me."

"Nigel has only looked over a couple of times. He's far too focused on Rachel to pay that much attention to you."

"If you say so." Olivia slid down in her seat and rested her knees on the back of the seat in front of her. She fidgeted in her seat, waiting for Fernando to come get her.

The surrounding crowd dwindled until it was just Sara, Mary, Hayley, and Olivia left waiting.

Olivia held her stomach. "My stomach is flipping. I feel like I'm about to get called to the principal's office."

Fernando walked down the aisle and led Sara to Tristan and Alex.

"You did nothing wrong. Why are you so nervous?"

"Alex thinks I did it. I told him I didn't, but he wouldn't listen. I don't know if Tristan believed me or not, but I can't blame him for siding with Nigel. Nigel's been his assistant cruise director for a long time. They're pretty close."

Fernando checked the list on his clipboard. He looked around the auditorium.

"We just need to figure out who actually did it."

"How are we supposed to figure that out?"

Fernando put his hand on Hayley's shoulder. "Tristan said that he knows where you were last night, so no need to stay. Sorry, I didn't let you know earlier."

"It's ok, Fern."

He turned to Olivia. "It looks like you are up."

Hayley stood up and grabbed Olivia's hand. "No worries, we'll head up."

Fernando's mouth hung open. "Hayley, I don't think..."

"I know. Tristan can tell me to my face if he wants me to leave."

Fernando shook his head and walked backstage.

"Are you sure you should go with me, Hayley? Won't that irritate Tristan when he had Fernando tell you that you could leave?"

Hayley linked arms with Olivia and led her up the aisle to the back of the auditorium. "He can be irritated if he wants to be. That's up to him. But I'm not abandoning you."

Alex watched the two of them walking toward them. He leaned towards Tristan and said something to him they couldn't hear. Both men sighed.

Olivia looked at Hayley, but Hayley held her head up high and looked directly at Tristan.

"Ladies." Tristan stood up and greeted them.

Hayley arched an eyebrow. "Gentlemen. You wanted to talk to us?"

"Actually, we wanted to speak with Olivia. Didn't Fernando tell you that you were free to leave?"

"He did." Hayley folded her arms and her chin jutted out.

Olivia recognized that look. She looked at Tristan. He sighed. Apparently, he recognized it, too.

"So, what have you two learned with your questioning?"

"Hayley, you know we can't tell you that."

"Fine. Let's go, Liv." Hayley put her hand on Olivia's back and steered her toward the door.

"Hold up." Tristan moved in between Hayley and the door. "We have a couple of questions for Olivia."

"She's told you both what she saw and that she didn't put Nigel in that truck. What else do you need to know?"

Alex rubbed his forehead and looked at Olivia. "Who knew that you were going to come back to the theatre last night?"

Olivia shrugged. "I don't know if anyone knew. I take that back. Tristan and Hayley knew."

"Did Nigel?"

Olivia looked at Hayley. "I don't think so. Did we say we needed to go back to the theatre?"

Hayley shrugged. "I don't think so. He knew we had stuff set up on stage, but

I don't think we said anything about having to go back and pack up."

"No, I don't think we did. At the same time, Hayley and I have been rehearsing after the last show a lot lately, so it wouldn't be surprising that someone would expect us to be there."

Alex stood up and the red velvet seat flipped up behind him. "I think that's all we need for now."

Tristan stood up next to him. "Thanks for answering our questions."

Hayley and Olivia looked at each other. "That's all?"

"Yep." Tristan looked at his watch. "I have to run. I'm hosting trivia in 20 minutes."

Tristan and Alex walked out of the theatre together.

"Did that seem too easy to you?"

"Thanks for helping me with my costume changes." Hayley pulled out the bobby pins holding her feathered headpiece on her head. She pulled the tight stocking cap that contained her hair off her head and sighed. "Oh, that feels better."

Olivia took the headpiece from her and put it on the shelf. "Happy to help. I honestly don't know how you all dance so effortlessly with those heavy things on your heads."

"You get used to it, I guess." Hayley sat down at her spot and unbuckled her silver shoe. "I'm glad we're getting a replacement dancer next cruise. Usually, they help me with my costume changes, but with the craziness of this cruise, Sara and Mary had their plates too full to help."

Olivia shrugged. "I enjoy helping. It's fun to be back here with the cast."

Rachel sank into her chair next to Hayley, unbuckled her shoe, and rubbed her foot.

Hayley rubbed her shoulders. "Are you okay, Rach?"

"Just worn out. I haven't missed that many shows, but I feel out of shape." Rachel took a long drink from her water bottle.

"Is your foot alright?"

"It's not hurt, I don't think. Just still tender."

Mary stood in front of the mirror, adjusting her dress.

Fernando knocked on the dressing room door. "Tristan wants everyone on stage in five."

Rachel opened up her bag and grabbed a pair of sweats. She pulled them on and slid her feet into her tennis shoes. Hayley pulled on her yoga pants and an oversized sweatshirt.

Rachel, Mary, Sara, Olivia, and Hayley walked out onto the stage. The heavy red velvet curtains were open and swayed on the edges of the proscenium.

Nigel helped Lorenzo get the plates and silverware off of his cart and onto the table they had set up, center stage.

"Nigel, do you need any help?" Mary asked.

He shook his head. "Nope, we've got it. Thanks."

"Okay." Mary sunk into one of the chairs set up on stage.

Hayley plopped on the stage floor. She opened her bag, pulled out her water bottle, and took a drink.

Nigel glared at Olivia.

Olivia knelt down next to Hayley. "Maybe I should head down to my cabin. Everyone would probably be more comfortable if I weren't here. Especially Nigel."

Haley took Olivia's hand and pulled her down onto the stage floor. "Don't be silly. You didn't do anything. If you leave every time Nigel is around, he'll think you are guilty. Just act normally."

"I don't know if I even know how to act normally."

"That's a point." Hayley grinned at her. "Just pretend for now."

The cruise staff began trickling into the theatre and came up on stage. They hovered around Lorenzo's cart, eyeballing the cake and chattering about their day.

The auditorium door opened and Tristan jogged down the aisle. He loosened his blue and gold striped tie and unbuttoned the top two buttons of his starched white dress shirt.

Tristan caught Hayley's eye and grinned.

He walked up to Lorenzo and put his hand on his shoulder. He leaned in and said something. Lorenzo nodded and took a step back from his cart, clasping his hands behind his back.

Olivia muttered. "I wish someone else had brought the cake. Lorenzo makes me nervous."

Hayley rolled her eyes. "Do you still think he killed Candi?"

"Maybe? Who else wanted Candi dead?" Olivia looked around at the rest of the entertainment department. She turned and Mary was looking right at her, her head cocked.

Mary glared at Olivia. "Why do you think someone wanted Candi dead? Maybe it was an accident?"

Tristan walked over to Nigel. He told him something and Nigel laughed. They patted each other on their backs.

Olivia turned back towards Mary. "Maybe you're right. But, Dr. Kohli thinks someone knew she was allergic to nightshades and gave her some. I don't know. It probably was an accident."

Lorenzo stood behind his cart, looking straight ahead.

"It just felt suspicious that Candi cheated on Lorenzo and Lorenzo was our waiter when Candi ate something she was allergic to."

Mary looked at Olivia. She shook her head, stood up, and walked over to Lorenzo.

Mary's face it up. She tossed her hair. Lorenzo grinned at her.

"Oh gosh. Are Lorenzo and Mary dating?" Olivia put her head down and covered her eyes. "I put my foot in my mouth saying that. Now Lorenzo is going to know what I said. I can't do anything right on this cruise. I'm going to be a pariah."

"You're not a pariah." Hayley smiled. "You have me. You can't get rid of me."

"I don't want to get rid of you, Hayley. You know that."

"You better not!"

Tristan took off his navy blazer and slid it over the back of a chair. He unbuttoned his cuffs and rolled them up.

Hayley tilted her head and sighed. "Oh my. Look at that. Who needs cake?"

Olivia laughed. "I've never seen you this taken with a guy."

"Have you seen the guy?"

"I have, actually."

"The hair, the body, that accent. He's nice and funny, too."

"So, when are you going to make your move?

"He's my boss, remember?"

"Technically, but it isn't like you are cruise staff and work directly under him.

I know staff members aren't supposed to date, but that doesn't stop anyone. Plus, you're an entertainer."

"Right, but unlike you, who is a headliner, and technically a passenger, I am on the crew manifest."

Olivia's jaw dropped."I didn't know that! That's not right. Especially since you are working on my show, as well as the production show."

"It doesn't bother me." Hayley shrugged. "I really enjoy being single, anyway. I don't need a boyfriend."

Tristan ran his hand through his blond hair.

"You can't keep your eyes off of him and he keeps looking at you."

"I see that." Hayley raised her eyebrow. "It feels good to know that I have his attention."

Tristan cleared his throat and stood up. "All right people. Before we dive into our sweet, I have an announcement to make."

A wave of chatter erupted in the crowd.

Tristan raised his hand to silence everyone. "I only told you half of the reason we're having a celebration tonight. Rachel, can you come up here with me?"

Lorenzo walked forward and handed them both a flute of champagne.

"Rachel, I talked with our Entertainment Director, Gayle Rogers, this morning and told her Dr. Kohli cleared you to resume performing. She wanted me to tell you how thrilled she is that you are healing."

The staff applauded for Rachel.

"She also wanted me to tell you she was very impressed with your performance the last time she saw the production show and she wants you to be the new dance captain."

Rachel gasped. "Oh, my goodness. This is only my second contract. I can't believe it!"

Nigel walked over and hugged Rachel. He draped his arm around her shoulders.

"Aw, good for Rachel. I'm so happy for her. I feel bad for Mary, though. She was hoping for that position."

Mary glared at Rachel. Her face had lost all color.

Lorenzo put his hand around her shoulder. She shook him off.

Tristan nodded to Lorenzo. "Ready for cake and champagne all around?"

Lorenzo picked up his knife and sliced the cake. He glanced to his left and right. Lorenzo noticed Olivia looking at him and paused. He stood taller and went back to slicing the cake.

Olivia looked away but watched him out of her side-line of sight.

Lorenzo picked up a piece of cake and slid it onto a plate. He took a step forward. Mary reached out and touched his arm. She said something to him and he handed her the plate.

Lorenzo cut another piece of cake and put it on a plate.

Mary turned away from the crowd, her body blocking Olivia's view of the cake. Mary reached into her pocket and pulled something out. She sprinkled something on the piece of cake. Mary turned back around and walked towards Rachel, a smile on her face. She walked up to Rachel and handed her the cake.

Mary lifted her hand to her mouth to lick the frosting off of her fingers and then froze. She lowered her hand and wiped it on her skirt.

Rachel looked around as if she needed something.

Mary turned towards the table set up in the middle of the stage. Her smile vanished as she turned away from

Rachel. She reached down and picked up a fork. She looked at Olivia, but her eyes looked right through her. A flash of a smirk crossed her face and her lip curled up.

Mary's eyes focused on Olivia, and she smiled.

Olivia attempted to smile back. Goosebumps raced up her arms.

Mary turned back towards Rachel. She handed Rachel the fork and walked back to Lorenzo.

Olivia stood up.

Rachel sunk the fork into her cake and lifted a bite to her mouth.

Olivia's hand shot up, covering her mouth.

"No!" Olivia screamed.

O livia raced across the stage and knocked the cake out of Rachel's hand.

Rachel's mouth hung open, her hand still holding the fork raised in the air.

Nigel grabbed Olivia's arm and twisted it behind her back. "What do you think you are doing?"

Hayley leapt off the ground. "Tristan!"

Tristan froze for a second and then reached down and pulled his radio off of his belt. Tristan pushed the button on his radio. "Charlie, Charlie, Charlie. Security needed on stage in the theatre." The squeal of the radio feeding back shot through the room.

"No, Tristan. Listen!" Olivia shouted. Olivia turned and looked at Hayley, begging her to intervene.

Hayley froze.

The theatre doors flew open. Alex and Victor sprinted down the aisle towards Tristan.

Alex scanned the stage and saw Nigel restraining Olivia. His eyes darted back and forth between Nigel to Olivia.

Olivia looked at him pleadingly.

"Tristan, what is going on here?" Alex asked.

Nigel cut Tristan off. "Olivia attacked Rachel. She hit her and knocked her cake out of her hands. I think she is the one that caused the accident that hurt Rachel and Kate."

"No!" Olivia's face lost all color. Her voice shook. "I didn't hurt Rachel and Kate. I am trying to protect Rachel."

Alex raised his hand to stop her from talking. He walked up to Nigel. "We're here. We've got her now."

Nigel released Olivia's arms. She rubbed the spot where he had held her. Victor gripped her shoulder.

"Alex. Let me explain." Tears fell down her cheeks.

The staff looked at her with appalled expressions. Rachel's eyes were wide and her chin trembled. Mary walked up next to Rachel and patted her back. She handed her a bottle of water. The lid was already off.

Olivia lurched out from Alex's grip. "No! Rachel, don't drink that!"

Alex caught her and pulled her back. "Olivia!" He wouldn't look at her.

"Rachel. I am not trying to hurt you. I am trying to protect you. Please." Tears streamed down Olivia's cheeks. "Please. I am begging you. Do not drink that water."

Nigel took the water bottle from Rachel. He sneered at Olivia. "Why? Did you poison it?"

"No! I didn't poison it. Mary did."

Everyone turned and looked at Mary.

Mary snorted. "Are you kidding me? Obviously, Olivia has a screw loose. She's dangerous. Can't you see it?"

"Check the cake." Olivia's voice cracked. "I saw her. She put something on it."

Alex nodded to Victor. Victor knelt down on the floor and examined the cake. He glanced up at Alex.

Alex gestured for Victor to come to him. He leaned into Victor and said something under his breath. Victor stepped forward and held Olivia's arm. Alex walked over to the spilled cake and knelt down. He examined the cake. He ran his finger through the frosting and held it up close to his face.

He looked up at Olivia.

Olivia held her breath, hoping he could see something on it.

Alex stood up and looked at Mary. He walked over to Lorenzo's cart and looked at the slices of cake sitting on it. He gestured for Tristan to join him.

Tristan leaned in and listened to Alex. He glanced at Olivia.

"It's berries, isn't it?" Olivia's breathing was shallow.

Tristan walked over to the spilled cake and knelt down. He looked at the cake on the floor and nodded to Alex.

"Olivia, you're right, there appears to be some kind of dried berries on Rachel's cake."

Olivia breathed a sigh of relief.

"How do we know you didn't put them there?" Alex asked.

Olivia's eyes widened. She spoke through her clenched teeth. "I wasn't anywhere near the cake."

She looked at Tristan. "Hayley can confirm that. We came out of the dressing room and sat on the stage floor. I saw Mary put something on it."

Hayley nodded. "That is true. Olivia sat next to me the entire time we were here. She never went near the cake."

"It was Lorenzo." Mary took a step back and pointed at him. "He must have put something on the cake."

Lorenzo's mouth gaped. "What?"

"After all, he's the one who was cutting it up and serving it." Mary shrugged. She looked into his eyes. "You did it, didn't you?"

"Why would I put something on Rachel's cake?" Lorenzo frowned.

"No!" Olivia pulled away from Victor.

Victor gripped her arm and pulled her close.

"How dare you accuse me of that? I would never." Lorenzo glared at Mary.

Olivia gasped. "It's not Lorenzo. He didn't do it. It was Mary. Mary poisoned Candi, too."

Olivia pointed at Mary. "You did it."

"I didn't do anything." Mary's eyes darted around the hushed crowd. "What? Why are you all looking at me like that?"

Olivia continued. "You put something on Rachel's cake. You tried to hide it, but I saw you do it."

Mary's eyes narrowed.

"You put whatever you gave Candi on Rachel's cake. You killed Candi. When she left, you thought you were going to be promoted to dance captain. You killed her."

"You have no proof."

Olivia looked towards the staircase, tucked behind the fly curtains. A flash of memory hit Olivia. She saw the card Chico had dropped to the floor. There had been grease on it.

Her eyes widened. "You hurt Kate and Rachel, too, didn't you?" Her head snapped back. "You put grease on the stairs so Kate would fall."

"Stop." Mary charged toward Olivia and grabbed her neck. She choked Olivia. "Don't say another word."

Victor pushed Mary away.

Olivia clutched her throat, gasping for air.

Alex took a step towards Mary, his arms outstretched, trying to grab her.

"Candi got what she deserved and you know it." Mary laughed. The sound of her laughter sent chills through Olivia. "You should thank me for getting rid of her after what she did to you."

"What she did to me?" Olivia rubbed her neck.

"She stole your boyfriend."

"Peter made the choice to go with her."

"Candi was a bad person. She cheated on Lorenzo. She stole my job from me."

"You killed her."

Mary's nostrils flared. "I didn't mean to kill Candi. I just didn't want her to take my job. She came back to the ship after Kate was out of my way and stole my job. I should have been dance captain, not her."

"You tried to poison Rachel. You put berries on her cake. Just like you put berries in Candi's cherries jubilee. You were trying to kill her, just like you killed Candi."

Rachel gasped. She leaned into Nigel. Nigel held her up.

Mary flipped around and glared at Rachel. "Oh, don't be a baby. You act like you're so perfect. But you knew how I felt about Nigel."

Rachel shook her head. "I had no idea. You never said anything."

Mary ignored her. She took a step towards Rachel. "That didn't stop you from making your moves on him. Then you took my rightful position as dance captain away from me. Candi was gone. Kate was gone. That job is mine."

Mary's eyes glazed over. She took another step toward Rachel.

Alex took his radio off his belt. It crackled with static. In a low voice, he said, "Alpha, Alpha, Alpha, Stage. Kohli, asap."

"But you couldn't leave well enough alone, could you?" Mary's voice was distant and flat.

Alex nodded to Victor. Victor dropped Olivia's arm and slowly walked toward Mary. Alex came at her from behind.

Mary glimpsed Alex behind her and took a step to the side. "I deserve to be dance captain. I've been dancing on ships longer than everyone else here."

"Mary, why did you put Nigel in my magic trunk?" Olivia held eye contact with her.

"It didn't hurt him. It just shook him up. He thought he could ignore me? He liked Rachel better than me?" Mary shifted her weight and pointed at Nigel. "How dare he not see what he was missing? No one saw what they were missing."

Mary lurched towards Lorenzo's cart and grabbed the knife he'd used to cut the cake. Her voice was shrill. "I deserve to be dance captain."

Alex crept up behind her.

Mary laughed.

Olivia shivered. She'd never heard a laugh like it before.

Mary raised the knife to her wrist. "What is the point if I'm not going to get any of the things I want?"

"Mary. Put down the knife." Tristan took a step towards Mary.

"Why should I?" Her lip curled in a snarl.

Mary lunged towards Tristan, jabbing the knife in his direction.

He jumped back, his hands raised.

Hayley sprang towards Tristan. Olivia grabbed her arm and pulled her back.

Alex's voice lowered. "Mary. It's alright. It's all over. Just put down the knife."

"I earned that spot."

"Of course you did." Alex reached his hand out toward Mary. "Give me the knife, Mary. Tristan will call Gayle. He'll talk to her about the dance captain position, won't you, Tristan?"

"Uh." Tristan rubbed the back of his neck.

"Won't you, Tristan." Alex arched his eyebrow.

Tristan nodded. "Of course. I'll call her as soon as you hand Alex the knife."

"You think I'm stupid?" Mary dodged Alex. She bolted upstage and grabbed Olivia.

Olivia gasped.

She held the knife to Olivia's throat.

Mary pulled Olivia back, knocking her off balance. "I know what you want to do to me. But it will not happen."

Mary's cold eyes looked through Alex. "If you take me down, she's going down with me. Call the Captain. I want a lifeboat ready for us. Once I'm on shore, I'll release her. Understand?" She yanked hard on Olivia's neck.

Alex nodded. "It's going to take a few minutes."

"I don't think you have a few minutes. If my lifeboat isn't ready and waiting for me when I get up to the Lido deck, she'll pay the price."

Olivia felt the cold steel of the knife against her neck. She swallowed, and the knife dug into her throat. She struggled to breathe.

Mary's voice rose in pitch. "I didn't mean to kill Candi. It was an accident. How was I supposed to know she was allergic to nightshades? The guy at the botanical garden just said it made people sick, you know? But now, you think I'm a murderer. I'm not. It's not my fault she died. Is it?" She dug the knife into Olivia's neck harder. A thin trickle of blood dripped down her neck. "Is it?"

Tears streamed down Olivia's cheeks. Olivia's voice was horse. "It's not your fault."

Alex took a step towards Mary and Olivia. "I'm sure you didn't mean it. Just a misunderstanding. Let's not make it worse, Mary. Let Olivia go."

Mary took the knife off of Olivia's neck and aimed it at Alex. "Stay back. I'm warning you!"

Alex's eyes darted over Mary's shoulder. He nodded.

Victor pulled out his stun gun and hit Mary on the arm with it.

Mary shrieked, and the knife clattered to the floor.

Victor pulled the stun gun away.

Mary gasped.

Alex pushed Mary towards Victor and pulled Olivia into his arms.

Victor put a handcuff on Mary's left hand and clamped it shut.

Mary kicked and screamed. She tried to pull her hand out of the handcuff.

He grabbed her other hand and pulled it behind her back. She lurched back, head butting him on the chin. Victor's head snapped back, blood dripping out of his mouth.

Dr. Kohli leapt forward and jabbed a needle into Mary's arm. "It's alright Mary, it's alright. You're just going to take a little nap."

Mary's hysterical sobs slowly faded as she went limp. Victor lowered her as she sank to the stage floor.

Alex held Olivia in his arms. He rocked her back and forth and kissed the top of her head.

Her tears soaked his white uniform shirt, her blood staining his shoulder.

"Sophie!" Olivia's voice was shrill. "I have to find my sub trunk. The show is tonight, and it isn't backstage. I can't find it anywhere."

"It's gone walkabout, has it?"

"Walkabout?"

"Sorry. Australia and the United States are two countries separated by a common language. I meant, has it taken off on you?"

"Alex, I mean Officer Ballas, took it when he was investigating the incident with Nigel. Victor says he brought it back, but it's not there."

"Alright, give me a few and I'll see if I can track that bugger down." Sophie picked up her phone. "I'll give you a ring when I find it."

Olivia blew Sophie a kiss. "Thank you."

Olivia raced backstage. "Hayley, any news on the trunk?"

Hayley shifted in her chair. "Sorry. I haven't heard anything."

Olivia's shoulder sank. She took a deep breath and exhaled. "Why? Why did this happen to me? It can't be that far. We're on a ship, for goodness' sake. It's not like it has that many places it could have gone."

Olivia sank down on the chair next to Hayley. She laid her head down on her folded arms on the shiny white counter of the makeup station. The heat from the lights surrounding the mirror made her neck hot. She leaned up and flipped the switch off.

"We'll find it."

"What if we don't?"

"We'll cross that bridge when we come to it." Hayley stood up and hung her costume on the rack. She glanced up at the clock. "Think it's time to tell Tristan?"

Olivia groaned. "I'm going to get kicked off the ship, aren't I? This is it. My bird keeps ruining the end of his new trick.

I've lost one of my props..... I thought we could do this show without Peter, but I don't know. Maybe I was wrong."

"Can't we pull out some of the stuff that you're giving to Peter when we get to port and use that if we can't find the sub trunk?"

"I already filled out the paperwork. They came and took it down to the hold so it'll be ready to get taken off when we get back to Canaveral."

"Could they have taken the sub trunk's case down into the hold with the other cases?"

Olivia's chin dropped. "Oh no! I bet that's where it is. We need to try to find it. Any idea how to get down into the hold?"

"I don't know where it is." Hayley shook her head. "Should we ask Tristan?"

"No, I don't want to freak him out about the show tonight. I'm hoping we can get this all fixed, and he doesn't have to know about it."

"Even if we could find it on our own, we wouldn't be able to carry it up to the theatre by ourselves. Alex is the one that took it. He should help us get it back."

Olivia crossed her arms. "I really don't want to talk to Alex."

"Why?" A smile crossed Hayley's face. "He was so sweet to you after they got Mary under control."

"I hate that I fell apart. It was so embarrassing. How could he think I had put Nigel in a trunk and that I hurt

Rachel?" Olivia's back sagged into her chair. "How could he think those things about me?"

"Let that go, Liv. It's his job to not believe anyone."

"I didn't do anything wrong, but I still feel mortified."

Hayley hugged Olivia. "You're right. You didn't do anything wrong. Let's go see Alex. We'll see if he can help us track down the trunk. Once you've talked to him this time, it'll make it easier in the future."

"I don't want to. I want to get off this ship and go..." Olivia froze.

"Go where, Olivia?" Hayley tilted her head and raised her eyebrows.

"I don't know. There is just so much pressure and nothing is going right." Olivia rested her hand on her stomach. "My stomach has been churning all day."

"Once we find the trunk and get this show out of the way, you will feel better. Let's go talk to Alex." Hayley reached down and held Olivia's hand. She pulled her towards the door of the dressing room.

They walked to Alex's office.

"Maybe I'll luck out and he won't be there."

"Do you want your trunk back or not?" Hayley stopped in the middle of the passageway, put her hands on her hips, and glared at Olivia.

"You're right. I need to suck it up." Olivia knocked on Alex's office door.

"Come in," Alex answered gruffly.

Olivia opened his door and took a step in.

Alex ran his fingers over his jaw. It was dark with 5 o'clock shadow. "Olivia. What brings you here? Oh, and Hayley, too." Alex stood up and gestured for them to take a seat.

Hayley slid past the first chair and plopped into the one tucked by the wall. Olivia perched on the edge of the first chair.

"My trunk is missing."

Alex cocked his head. "Sorry, I've had a long couple of days. Can you remind me what trunk you're talking about?"

"The trunk you took. The one you thought I put Nigel in."

Alex's head tilted back and a slight smile passed over his lips.

"It's not funny, Alex."

"Sorry. Didn't mean to imply that I was amused." Alex squared the pile of paper he'd been working on and moved it to the corner of his desk. "I had Victor bring your trick back and put it in the wings."

"It's not there. I talked to Victor. He went to look and said it wasn't where he had put it." Olivia threw up her hands. "I've looked all over the theatre."

"Did you ask Fernando if he has seen it?"

"Of course we did. I even got Fernando to take me into the storage area under the stage behind the pit. We can't find it anywhere."

"I'll put word out. I'm sure it will turn up." Alex slid the pile of paperwork back to the center of his desk.

"No! That's not good enough. We have a show in..." Olivia looked at her watch. "Three hours. I need my trunk back and I need it now."

"Alright, calm down."

Olivia's eyes widened. She took a deep breath and let it out. "We think that the trunk might have been taken down into the hold with the other travel cases that are getting signed off when we get back to Canaveral. I don't know where they store them once they pick them up from backstage. Do you?"

Alex nodded. "Let me see what I can do."

He picked up the phone and spoke to someone on the other end. He nodded his head. "Kalá."

Alex hung up the phone. "He's going to get his team to look. He'll call me back when they have a chance." Alex leaned back in his chair.

"Are you kidding me?" Olivia slammed her hands onto Alex's desk. "You don't seem to understand the urgency here. In less than three hours, I am going to be standing on stage trying to entertain 1,500 guests. If I don't have my trunk back by then, I don't have a closing for my show. And I won't have 45 minutes of material to do. The show will be a disaster. Tristan will fire me."

Alex raised his hand. "Ok, calm down."

"Calm down? How dare you tell me to calm down?" Olivia's nostrils flared. "You did this. You are the one who took my trunk. When I did nothing wrong! I told you I hadn't put Nigel in the trunk, but you didn't believe me. And now you've lost it. It is all your fault that I am in this position."

Hayley put her hand on Olivia's shoulder and patted her. "Liv. Give Alex a chance to make this right. You are going to make this right, aren't you, Alex?"

"Of course." Alex rubbed the back of his neck. "Olivia, what do you want me to do?"

Olivia cleared her throat. "I want you to take us down into the hold and help us look for my trunk. If it isn't there, I want you to keep looking until you find it."

Alex glanced at the pile of paperwork on his desk and sighed. He turned the pile over, facedown on his desk. He stood up and waved towards the door. "Ladies."

Hayley and Olivia walked out into the corridor. Alex shut his office door. He turned towards them and looked at their sandals. "Are you sure you don't want me to go to the hold and look and come find you after? You aren't even wearing real shoes. It a lot rougher down there than what you are used to."

"We're not delicate flowers, Alex. We'll be fine."

"Don't say I didn't warn you." Alex headed down the corridor and pushed open a door to the crew area. He held it open for Olivia and Hayley to walk through. He turned the corner and headed down the steps.

Olivia's hand slid down the smooth wood banister. Alex peeled off the stairs and headed towards the main corridor.

Metal carts, bins, and pallets of stuff wrapped in plastic-lined the passageway. Crew members rushed in both directions, some pushing carts.

Olivia wrinkled her nose. It smelled like industrial cleaner.

Olivia's eyes darted back and forth as she looked into the rooms on both sides of the passageway. Framed announcements hung on the walls. One invited the crew to a tropical themed party at the crew bar, another reminded them of the upcoming cabin inspections. Olivia breathed a sigh of relief that she was in a passenger cabin and didn't have to worry about cabin inspections.

A chef in his tall white hat and a group of deckhands in blue overalls passed by them. Alex nodded a greeting to them. Olivia moved behind Hayley as the corridor narrowed from bundles of cardboard boxes lining the walls.

Olivia stopped dead in her tracks and sniffed. "What the heck is that?"

Alex looked over his shoulder.

He glanced around. "Ah, that smell? The incinerator room is coming up. It is where all the burnable trash is taken."

"Yuck." Olivia pulled the front of her shirt up over her nose.

"Necessary." Alex turned and continued walking towards the aft of the ship." It's not all glamorous on the ship."

"I realize that, Alex. I just never thought about what happened to all the garbage."

The hallway opened up. On the port side of the ship, there was a prep kitchen. The floor of the hallway had a puddle of water. At least Olivia hoped it was water. Bits of produce floated in the liquid. Hayley and Olivia walked carefully through, trying not to get their feet too wet.

Alex continued down the long corridor.

"Here is the marshaling area. Your trunk is most likely down here somewhere."

Olivia looked around the enormous space, crowded with stuff. There were stacks of pallets, large boxes filled with recyclables, empty luggage carts, and crates stacked to the ceiling. One wall was lined with small forklifts.

Olivia heard the hiss of steam and water surging through the pipes overheard in the low ceiling.

"How on earth are we going to find my trunk mixed in with all of this stuff? I still need to get the rest of the show preset, too." She looked down at her watch and shook her head. "Oh shoot! I forgot to take Chico's food dish out of his cage. He is more motivated for his treats when he hasn't been eating in a couple of hours before the show."

"That makes me more motivated, too." Alex chuckled. "Believe it or not, while this area looks like chaos, it is all very well organized. These guys know where everything is. When we get into port, they have to get everything moved out of the ship and all the fresh supplies moved onto the ship in less than eight hours. No one on the ship is more organized than this team. Isn't that right, gentlemen?"

Three men in uniform were talking, clipboards in hand.

"That's right Ballas. What brings you down here?"

"These young ladies have misplaced a trunk they use in their show. We think it might have been brought down here.

They are hoping you can help them find it."

Olivia looked at her watch. "I should have stayed down there with Alex until he got someone to bring the trunk backstage."

"Livvy, calm down. Alex said he'd get it backstage in time for the show. He needed to track down someone who could move it. You needed to get Chico and get started presetting the show. It would have been silly for you to just stand there and watch him."

"Snack!" Chico bobbed his head up and down.

"Buddy, you'll get snacks soon. I promise." Olivia put the deck of cards on the velvet table top and put it in its spot in the stage left wing. "What are the chances you are going to do your new trick properly, bird?"

Chico rocked back and forth in his travel carrier. "E, I, E I, quack, quack, quack, O!"

Olivia shook her head. "You are a pip today, aren't you?"

"La, la, la," Chico dropped an octave for his last la. "laaaa...."

Olivia lifted the black cover and pulled it over his cage. He muttered to himself. She heard him making his sleepy sounds. "Good, maybe he'll take a nap before the show."

"He's full of it tonight, isn't he?" Hayley giggled.

"Let's see if you are still laughing when you are on stage with him doing your songs together and he does this ridiculousness."

"It'll be fine. No matter what he does, he's adorable and everyone will love him."

Olivia opened up the bag with the linking rings and pulled them out. She organized them and put them back in the bag.

"You've done that three times already, Liv." Hayley squeezed Olivia's shoulders. "It's going to be just fine. I promise."

Victor and Alex came through the stage door. They had Olivia's sub trunk on a low-wheeled cart and were bent over, pushing it. "We couldn't find anyone to help us get it up here, so we found this cart and brought it up ourselves."

Oliva exhaled. She closed her eyes and her head tilted forward. "What a relief!"

"Where do you want it?"

"Stage right. The stage crew will take it from there."

"Stage right?" Alex cocked his head.

"Sorry, over there." Olivia pointed to the far side of the stage. She rushed across the stage as the guys lifted the trunk off the cart. She walked around the trunk and inspected it, then lifted the lid and looked inside. "Oh! Thank goodness. The handcuffs and the bag are in there. I was worried they were lost."

Alex grinned. "Glad it's all there. Need anything else?"

Olivia's shoulders relaxed, and she smiled. "No. That is all I need. Thank you."

"Sorry for the problems."

Olivia shrugged. "It's over now." She looked at her watch. "Oh boy, I need to get changed."

"Break a leg tonight." Alex laughed. "Did I get that right? It doesn't sound like a good thing to say."

"You got it right." Olivia smiled. "And yes, it's good luck."

Olivia picked up Chico's carrier and raced to the dressing room. She threw on her costume for the opening number. She and Hayley were touching up their hair and makeup when Tristan knocked on the dressing room door.

"Five minutes to curtain."

"We're ready."

They followed him on stage and took their places.

Fernando handed Tristan his microphone. The stage curtains pulled apart a couple of feet and then closed behind Tristan as he walked out on stage to the applause of the audience.

Hayley and Olivia stood on the dimly lit stage. Hayley's long leg jutted through the slit in her silver gown. Olivia stood with one hand raised in the air.

They heard Tristan wrap up their introduction. The curtain opened as Tristan said, "Olivia Morgan, and Hayley!"

The light of the follow spot hit their silver dresses. Flashes of light bounced off of the sequins. The audience clapped as Olivia threw a flash of fire and Chico appeared. She walked to the apron of the stage and put Chico on his ring stand. He rocked back and forth on his swing. Hayley and Olivia finished the opening number to applause.

Olivia walked forward as the curtain closed behind her.

She introduced Chico and his new trick. Her hands were sweaty, and the cards were sticking to her fingers as she tried to shuffle them. She lifted Chico off of his stand and put him on the velvet-covered table.

She pulled three cards out of the deck of cards and laid them on the table in front of Chico.

She lifted the center card and showed him, and the audience, the Ace of Spades. Olivia put it back on the table, facedown. She slowly moved the three cards and then picked up the pace until it seemed impossible that anyone would know which card was the Ace of Spades.

Olivia stood back and nodded to Chico. She held her breath as he walked forward and looked at the backs of the three cards. He cocked his head and looked over at Olivia. He looked back at the cards, took a step forward, and picked up one card. It was the Ace of Spades.

Chico held it in his beak.

Olivia took the card from his beak and held it up for the audience to see.

The audience clapped.

Chico flapped his wings, and he bobbed his head up and down.

"Good boy!" Olivia picked him up and held him on her hand. Olivia reached in her pocket and pulled out a sunflower seed.

"Snack!" Chico ate the seed as Hayley walked out and took him from Olivia. She carried him backstage as Olivia introduced the next trick.

The rest of the show flew by.

Behind Olivia, the stage crew pulled the sub trunk onto the stage and locked the castors. Olivia looked into the wings and checked to make sure Hayley was ready. Hayley gave her a thumbs up. Olivia cued Fernando to start the music.

Hayley spun onto the stage in a slinky red mini dress.

Olivia lifted the lid to the trunk and stepped in. Hayley put the handcuffs on Olivia and pulled the bag up over her as Olivia sank down into the trunk. Hayley shut the lid and jumped on top of the trunk. She raised the curtained hoop up to her waist.

"1……2…" Hayley shouted. She lifted the hoop over her head and then dropped it.

"3!" Olivia shouted, standing on top of the trunk where Hayley had just been. She jumped off the trunk, opened the lid, and Hayley, inside the bag, stood up. Olivia untied the bag and Hayley popped out, now wearing a purple dress.

The audience gasped and clapped. Olivia helped Hayley out of the trunk, and they both ran to the front of the stage and took a bow. They backed up, and the curtain closed in front of them.

Tristan announced their names again, and the curtain re-opened. Hayley and Olivia walked forward, this time with Chico perched on Olivia's hand. They took their final bows and ran backstage. The curtain whooshed shut behind them.

"We did it." Hayley raised her hand and clapped Olivia's hand with a high five. "I gotta be honest. I was really worried that we hadn't been able to do a full run-through before the show."

"You said you weren't nervous at all." Olivia's eyes widened.

"If I had said I was nervous, you would have been a wreck. I'm just so glad it all went well."

"Me, too." Olivia exhaled. "So relieved."

"Snack?!" Chico yelled from his perch on the back of Olivia's chair.

"Yes, sir!" Olivia looked for her bag that had Chico's treats. "Uh oh. I think I left it in the cabin."

"Uh oh!" Chico rocked back and forth. "Oh, no!"

Someone knocked on their dressing room door. "Are you decent? Can I come in?"

"Yes, we're dressed. Come on in, Alex."

"I saw the show. You both did an excellent job. Chico, too."

"Snack?"

"Actually, Chico, I brought you a snack. As long as Olivia says it is ok, of course." Alex pulled out a bag of cherries. "I had some at dinner tonight and thought of my favorite parrot friend. Lorenzo put them in a bag for me so I could bring them to him."

"That was very thoughtful of you. And of Lorenzo." Olivia shrugged. "He wouldn't eat the cherries I brought him a couple of days ago, so don't feed bad if he won't eat them."

Alex opened the bag and pulled out a cherry. He offered it to Chico.

"Mmmm." Chico took the cherry and held it with his foot as he dug into it. His light-colored beak was covered with red cherry juice.

"He looks like he belongs in a horror movie, with blood dripping from his beak."

Alex laughed and handed him another cherry.

Chico dropped the pit from the first cherry on the floor and grabbed the second cherry out of Alex's hand.

"Mmmm. Treat!"

Nigel knocked on the dressing room door. "Um, Olivia. Can I come in?"

Olivia's eyes widened. "Of course."

"I came to apologize."

"You have nothing to apologize for."

Nigel shuffled his feet. He looked up at Olivia. "I shouldn't have thought that you shoved me in the trunk. I knew it was out of character for you, but I was so shaken...."

Olivia walked over to Nigel. "Of course, it shook you up. You must have been terrified, trapped in my trunk. I was upset that you thought I would do such a thing, but I understand why you did. No hard feelings, okay?"

"That's a relief. Thank you."

O livia grabbed her tote bag and patted her pocket to make sure she had her wallet. She glanced at her watch. She was running late to meet Hayley at the gangway.

"See you later, Chico."

"While, crocodile."

"Close enough. I'm going to the pet store today, so I'll have goodies for you when I get back from running my errands."

"Oh, boy!"

Olivia raced down to the gangway.

Victor and Alex were standing at the entrance.

"Alex, did you see if they got Peter's cases offloaded?" Olivia's eyes flitted around the dock, looking for the cases.

"I did." Alex looked at his watch. "They took them off and put them in the terminal about forty-five minutes ago."

Olivia exhaled. "Phew. Glad that is over with."

"What are you up to today?" Alex asked.

"Hayley and I rented a car. We're driving into Orlando so we can pick up some supplies and stop at the pet store."

"That will please, Chico."

"Oh, yes!"

"Hayley came through about five minutes ago"

"Yeah, I was running late, so she said she'd go ahead and get the paperwork filled out for the rental."

"Enjoy your day."

"Thanks!" Olivia stepped onto the gangway and carefully walked down the steep metal ramp, holding the handrails. She crossed the dock and headed into the crew entrance of the terminal. She heard Hayley laugh and scanned the room, looking for her.

Olivia spotted Hayley's copper hair and headed toward her. Hayley's shoulders were shaking. She gasped a big breath of air and let out a cackle of laughter.

Olivia smiled, wondering what was making her friend laugh so hard. "Hayley!"

Hayley turned towards Olivia and then took a step to the side.

Peter was standing there. He was smiling at Hayley like they were old friends.

Olivia felt gutted that her friend was talking and laughing with Peter after what he had done to her. She slowed her step; her smile crumpled.

"Liv. Guess what?"

Olivia's brow furrowed and she pinched her lips together. "What?"

"Peter got a contract on another ship."

"Good for him." Olivia avoided looking at Peter.

Hayley grinned. "Guess what the best part is?"

"We really don't have time for guessing games. We need to pick up the rental."

"I've already got the keys." Hayley's mouth curled up in a half-smile. "Ok, fine. I won't make you guess. Peter tracked me down. He offered me a job."

"A job?"

Peter stepped towards Olivia. "There is no way I could work with you after how you treated me. So I have offered Hayley the position as my assistant. Since she has been helping you out with your little act, I thought she would appreciate the opportunity to work with a real magician. One with years of experience headlining shows."

Olivia looked at Hayley. Hayley looked back with a grin on her face.

Olivia put her hand on her stomach. She felt like someone had punched her in the gut. "Hayley?"

"We all know you aren't going to be able to pull off your little show long-term. She'd be out of a job if she tied herself to you." Peter raised his chin. "Obviously, I have more to offer her than you do."

Olivia clenched her jaw.

"So, what do you think?" Hayley asked.

"What do I think? I mean, it is your career. You have to choose what you want to do." Olivia's stomach fluttered.

"No, no, no." Hayley shook her head. She ran her hand down her face. "What do you think about this arrogant...

reprobate? He actually thought I would abandon you for him."

Hayley burst into laughter. Tears fell down her cheeks, and she gasped for air.

Relief washed over Olivia.

Peter's nostrils flared. "Hayley. I am going to give you one more opportunity to make the right choice."

Hayley wheezed with laughter. She bent over and put her hand on her side.

Hayley handed Olivia the rental car keys. "Here, you had better drive. I can't stop laughing. Let's go get some magic supplies. We have a show to do."

Hayley put her arm around Olivia's shoulder and walked her out to the parking lot.

Book 1

Book 2

Book 3

Coming Fall 2022.

Join my mailing list at

https://wendyneugent.com/

to be alerted to new releases.

Wendy Neugent spent close to a decade as part of an award-winning magic act performing on cruise ships all over the world. She traveled from Alaska to Venezuela, Bermuda to Tahiti, and many exotic ports of call in between.

Now, Wendy uses her insider's knowledge of cruise ship life to write fun and entertaining cozy mystery books set on cruise ships.

Wendy's Cruise Ship Mysteries are the perfect books to read while taking a cruise or when you wish you were on vacation.

https://wendyneugent.com/

Made in the USA
Middletown, DE
29 November 2024